'19

YOURS FOR ETERNITY

Danielle McMasters was haunted by the memory of the man she had loved and lost in a fatal car crash six years before. Ben was dead. So who, then, was the man watching her from across the room? His likeness was uncanny — it had to be Ben . . . hadn't it? But how could he have returned from the grave — and why was someone following her every move? The past was haunting her present, but how would it affect her future?

Books by Janet Whitehead
in the Linford Romance Library:

FAR EASTERN PROMISE
A TIME TO RUN

JANET WHITEHEAD

YOURS FOR ETERNITY

Complete and Unabridged

LINFORD
Leicester

First published in Great Britain in 1991

First Linford Edition
published 2007

British Library CIP Data

Whitehead, Janet
   Yours for eternity.—Large print ed.—
Linford romance library
1. Love stories
2. Large type books
I. Title
823.9′14 [F]

ISBN 978–1–84617–947–1

Published by
F. A. Thorpe (Publishing)
Anstey, Leicestershire

Set by Words & Graphics Ltd.
Anstey, Leicestershire
Printed and bound in Great Britain by
T. J. International Ltd., Padstow, Cornwall

This book is printed on acid-free paper

Dedicated to a real character —
Aunt Nell

1

'Really, Dani,' said Barbara Summers, studying the object of her admiration through large tinted glasses. 'I just don't know how you do it.'

The flame-haired fashion editor of *Latest* magazine was referring to the winter collection Danielle McMasters had just unveiled in the plush conference suite of the Playfair Hotel, in the heart of London's West End.

'The designs are bold and innovative, the materials reflect care and attention, and the prices . . . well, what can I say? You're putting the latest and most exclusive fashions within the reach of every woman — yet again.'

Barbara took a sip from her champagne glass and glanced quickly around the crowded room, then leaned forward to ask with a frown, 'How *do* you do it?'

Dani McMasters chuckled warmly. A

tall, slim twenty-seven-year-old with a graceful, flowing neck, finely sculpted features and a 'tousled and textured' cut to her short, butter-coloured hair, she enjoyed the praise — but no amount of flattery would get her to reveal the secrets of her hard-earned success.

'You wouldn't believe me if I told you,' she replied, sipping from her own glass.

'Try me.'

Dani feigned mock horror. 'What, and have my competitors read all about it in your magazine?'

'As if I'd do that to you.'

'You mean to say that you wouldn't?'

The two women exchanged a shrewd and meaningful look. Each knew how fiercely competitive the world of fashion could be, just as both were aware of how jealously sought-after was Dani's expertise in finding — and encouraging — the best new designers around.

She had virtually revolutionized the High Street fashion business in the last four years, bringing the finest of clothes to the thirty-five retail outlets of Beau Monde, the company for whom she worked as chief fashion buyer.

Thanks to a fresh approach and an apparently tireless dedication, she had been able to present season after season of exciting collections to an eager and increasingly clothes-conscious public, and even more incredibly, to sell these designer fashions at mass-market prices.

But whilst her bosses made no secret of their admiration for her, she had also made enemies.

Malcolm Bradbury, managing director of rival clothing chain Yours, for example. Every three months for the last two years he had tried to woo her away from Beau Monde. Just last week he had practically offered her a blank cheque if she would go to work for him, and taken her subsequent refusal as a personal insult.

That meeting had quickly turned nasty, she reflected, and she had left Bradbury's office for the watery April sunshine outside with more than a little relief. Still, at least the short, one-sided argument had resolved the situation once and for all. She didn't think it likely that he would ever ask her to join him again, and was glad.

Even so, it irritated her that he couldn't — or wouldn't — understand that her interests lay not in the promise of a high salary and an endless procession of top-range company cars, but simply in *fashion*, good, durable *fashion*, and the fostering of talented young designers who would always be the future of her business.

And in any case, she owed too much to Colin Howard and the others at BM to leave them now. They had been good to her when she had needed them most, and gave her as much freedom as she required to do her job. She was happy there and had no particular desire to move on.

'You don't like us much, do you?' Barbara said suddenly, breaking into her thoughts.

Dani blinked rapidly as the surrounding babble of conversation came back up to full volume. 'I'm sorry?'

'Journalists,' the other woman explained, nibbling at a canapé. 'You always appear very wary of us.'

'Oh, I wouldn't say that exactly.'

'Really? Then you're being as diplomatic as ever, darling.'

Dani's smile revealed white, even teeth. 'Well, let's just say that there are reporters, and there are reporters — if that makes any sense.'

'Once bitten, twice shy?' Barbara prompted.

'That's one way of putting it.'

A stunningly attractive woman in her late thirties, Barbara was a former gossip columnist with an awesome reputation for thorough, no-holds-barred journalism. Now, noting a subtle shift in both Dani's tone and manner, and sensing a story there somewhere, she frowned and tilted her head to one side, softening her voice deliberately as she said, 'They gave you a bad time, didn't they? About six years ago?'

Dani ran her hazel eyes over the people clustered at the buffet tables and nodded, obviously uncomfortable with the subject. 'Yes,' she replied softly, 'they did.'

'So you've been cautious of them ever since?'

'To be honest, Barbara, I really haven't given it much thought.'

'Wasn't it something to do with an accident?' the fashion editor said, her frown deepening as she tried to dredge up half-remembered trade-paper head-lines. 'A car?'

Now Dani was visibly ill at ease. 'Yes. But it was a long time ago and — '

'A man . . . ' Barbara cut in. 'His name started with a *t*, I think. Tr . . . Tremain, was it?'

'Yes.' The word came out sharper than intended, almost making the other woman flinch. Dani took a deep, steadying breath and willed a smile back onto her face. 'I . . . I'm sorry, Barbara. You'll have to forgive me, but I really don't want to talk about it.'

'Even now?' Barbara persisted. 'Six years later?'

'Yes. Even now.'

The reporter smiled. Her instincts told her that there was definitely a story to be found here, but she knew from experience that she would get nothing more from Dani herself. For that she would have to approach other sources.

'I understand, love,' she said, switching on her kindest tone. 'And I apologize. Just can't stop prying, I suppose. Must be in my blood.'

'Well, that's what you're paid for.'

'That's what I *used* to be paid for,' Barbara corrected. 'These days I only write about fashion.'

Seeing a chance to change the line of conversation, Dani asked, 'And what *will* you be saying about the collection you've just seen?' She took another sip from her glass, hoping that the other woman wouldn't notice the trembling of her hand.

'I'll tell the truth, of course,' Barbara

replied with an easy smile. 'That once again, the phenomenal Danielle McMasters has made the good name of Beau Monde synonymous with everything that is tasteful and stylish.'

'That's what I was hoping you'd say,' Dani said, regaining control of herself. 'Now, you really must excuse me, Barbara. As nice as it is to see you, I really *must* mingle.'

'Of course, I understand.'

As Dani moved away, Barbara Summers studied her through narrowed, thoughtful eyes. What was she hiding? What was it about her past that she had chosen to bury?

* * *

As she moved among the other elegantly-attired guests, Dani's heartbeat slowly returned to normal and the high colour left her face. Before long, she had calmed down enough to return the smiles offered her with some semblance of sincerity, and accept congratulations on the presentation with appreciative nods.

Still, it was strange how those terrible events of six years before continued to affect her. No matter how many times she tried to block them from her mind, some*thing*, or some*one*, always brought them back.

'Great show, Dani. Really enjoyed it.'

'Thank you, Alex.'

'Oh, Miss McMasters — any chance of talking to you about the Petersen designs?'

'Certainly. Just give me five minutes and I'll be right with you.'

Almost without exception, the guests attending both the show and its reception were connected with the fashion business in some way. Not only were all the major trade and women's magazines represented, but she was also gratified to see a large contingent of foreign buyers, to whom Dani's colleagues would later be trying to sub-license the designs on show here today.

Now Dani moved among them completely at ease, and with a co-ordinated flow that hinted at her previous career as a fashion model. Indeed, due to a strict regime of diet and exercise, her body, beneath a black and red velveteen cotton and acetate dress, was as sleek and perfect now as it had been at the height of her photographic career.

Neither had the years left many marks on her smooth face. Fine brows arched delicately above her dark, glowing eyes, and her nose, set above full, sensuous lips, was appealingly snubbed.

She was, in fact, a very beautiful girl who had grown into a very beautiful woman, and like all such women, she was secretly very, very lonely.

A smartly-dressed waiter crossed her path, carrying a tray filled with Stilton-stuffed eggs. They looked delicious, but she had no appetite. To her left, someone said something amusing and the people around him laughed.

Just glancing around, she smelled a dozen different perfumes on the warm, slightly stuffy air, all of them mingling with cigar smoke and the heady scents of champagne and sherry.

Dani suppressed a grimace. She didn't really care for these affairs at all, just as she was never totally comfortable with all the glitz that went into the launching of a new collection. But, as she had learned long ago, it was a necessary evil. A vast amount of Beau Monde's business was generated by these trade shows, so they were vital not only in promoting new designers, but also for the company's continued growth.

Today, however, she just didn't seem to have the patience for it. Perhaps her emotions were beginning their climb-down after all the hype that went on before the show. That had happened many times before. Or perhaps Barbara Summers had stirred up more memories in her than she'd realized.

'Dani! *Dani!*'

She turned just as a tall young man in a pale-grey suit and open-necked blue shirt edged through the crowd towards her.

David Mason was a handsome twenty-three-year-old with a clear, tanned skin and the most exquisite green eyes. He was easily the most gifted designer Dani had ever worked with, but when she had first discovered him a year before, he'd been working as a male model to supplement his meagre allowance as a student. Today had marked his second appearance at a Beau Monde fashion show, and, as with that first time, his lacy, romantic — but incredibly practical — creations had caused quite a stir.

At the sight of him, a smile spread quickly across her face. 'David! I'm sorry, we didn't get the chance to speak before the show.'

'Well, we *were* rather busy,' he replied, grinning at the understatement.

She laughed. 'Do you think it was worth it, though?'

The young man's nod was emphatic, and sent a shiver through his shoulder-length salt-and-pepper hair. 'The whole thing was just fabulous, even watching from the wings as I was. It just came together perfectly.' He glanced around. 'The buyers were impressed as well. Colin tells me that the crowd from De Sala in Paris want to take six of my designs.'

Her eyes lit up with genuine pleasure. 'That's marvellous,' she said sincerely, taking his right hand and squeezing it. 'I'm so glad for you, David, because you really deserve it.'

He shrugged, obviously embarrassed. 'Well, I don't know about that. And in any case, it's still early days yet.'

'Maybe — but it's no mean achievement when an Englishman sells fashion to the French.'

He chuckled.

'Have you got a drink?' she asked.

'Just on my way to get one,' he replied. 'But I wanted to tell you the good news fir — Dani, are you all right?'

Her gaze had wandered slightly, to focus on something behind him, and her eyes suddenly widened as all the colour drained from her cheeks.

David stepped closer, his face a mask of concern. 'Dani, what's wr — '

Her single, mumbled word interrupted him. 'N — no . . . '

As he took her by the arms she shook her head and said it again. Then her dark eyes locked with his and he saw confusion, fear and disbelief battling each other within them.

She whispered, 'It . . . it *can't* be . . . '

Suddenly she tried to push past him, as if to get to whoever was standing behind him, dropping her champagne glass in the process.

'Dani!' he cried, tightening his grip on her.

But still she continued her struggle to get past, aware only of whatever lay beyond him.

Now those guests nearest them turned to stare at her. The buzz of conversation began to die, the large room to quieten.

'What the — '

'What's happening?'

Then Dani felt the sickening mixture of wine, smoke and perfume begin to crowd her senses. From white, her face went quickly back to red. She looked hot and agitated, blinked several times in quick succession, muttered a name —

'Ben . . . '

— and then her eyes rolled up into her head and her legs turned to water.

'*Dani!*'

The name echoed in her ears. *Dani . . . Dani . . . Dani . . .*

Then she collapsed.

*   *   *

When she opened her eyes again, she saw a plain white ceiling.

She blinked slowly, with effort, until her hazel eyes cleared enough to focus on a small hairline crack running from the corner of the overhead fluorescent light strip.

She felt tired and weak, disoriented. She just wanted to go back to sleep. But a vague sense of unease kept nagging at her. Something had happened. Something important. What?

Carefully she turned her head to find that she was in a small, bright room. There were no windows, and it was consequently very quiet.

Where was she?

A large, locked cupboard upon which had been stencilled a red cross caught her eye, and she frowned. There was something about that red cross that triggered odd, indistinct memories within her. Something about . . .

Then she had it.

The presentation, the reception —

The reception!

She had been lying on a narrow cot. Now she sat up abruptly, then froze, moaning at the needling pain in her head.

'Dani, thank God!'

'What — !'

She jumped, startled, as a raven-headed

16

woman about four years her junior rose from a chair beside the room's single door.

Kathrine Allison was her deputy at Beau Monde, a tall, lithe woman with strong, confident features who wore her black hair in a wild, shaggy style that perfectly matched the predatory look in her gold-flecked eyes.

Now, however, those eyes showed nothing but concern as she hurriedly crossed the room to ease Dani back onto the cot.

'Kate, what — '

'All right, Dani, all right. Take it easy.'

'But — '

'Shhh.'

Reluctantly Dani set her head back against the soft pillow and stared up at her long-time friend and colleague.

'How do you feel?' Kate asked softly.

Dani frowned. Good question, she thought. Reaching up, she set a palm against her forehead. She was cool now, cooler than she had been, and apart from the headache and a slight, lingering threat of nausea, better. She said as much, adding, 'Kate — what happened?'

'You fainted.'

'Fai — ' Quickly Dani glanced around the small room, her expression asking the question.

'You're in the hotel rest-room,' Kate replied. 'When you passed out, all hell broke loose, if you'll pardon my language. David panicked. Colin started having kittens. I thought you were dead drunk — '

'Kate!'

'Only joking,' Kate smiled. 'Anyway, David scooped you up and he and the manager brought you here, then someone called a first-aider who came in to give you a quick once-over. She said that you'd probably passed out because it was so stuffy in the conference suite, and would probably sleep for about fifteen or twenty minutes.' Her golden eyes fell to her expensive Tissot wrist-watch. 'She was right.'

But as Kate explained everything to

her, Dani's frown deepened instead of eased. Fainted? She'd never fainted in her life, was as strong as an ox. Her eyes narrowed still further as she tried to recall the events which had led to her passing out.

Only blurred images would come to mind at first, brief, infuriating snatches of memory. Her headache grew worse, but she persevered. The more she concentrated, the sharper the memories became.

She had been talking with David. That was right. He had been saying something about De Sala, the famous French fashion house, when she had happened to glance over his shoulder and seen —

Suddenly it all came back. *Everything*. Kate saw as much on her face.

'Dani — what is it? You've gone as white as a sheet!'

Indeed she had. Looking up at Kate now, she felt as if she might faint again, but somehow held on to consciousness and breathed, 'Kate, I've got to talk to

Colin. Can you . . . will you get him for me? Please?'

Kate nodded, obviously mystified. 'Of course. He's right outside. But shall I — '

'Please. I'll be all right. But I must speak to Colin.'

No more than ten seconds passed before the rest-room door opened again and a slightly overweight man in his late thirties looked in on her. His face had a smooth, red look, as if it had recently been scrubbed, and his hair was short and greying.

'Dani? Are you — ?'

'Colin, come in, please.'

Colin Howard did as she asked, closing the door softly behind him. The managing director of Beau Monde was dressed in a conservative grey suit, white shirt and blue tie. He looked inoffensive, almost mousy, as he crossed the small room, but in fashion circles his professionalism was almost legendary.

Colin and his wife Sandra had

opened their first shop in Exmouth in 1974, catering mainly to the tourist trade, and the business had expanded from there. Today annual turnover was within the region of a million to a million and a half pounds.

'How are you?' he asked, taking one of her hands. 'You gave us quite a scare, I can tell you.'

She looked up into his anxious face, trying desperately to find some comfort there. Licking her lips, she said softly, 'I saw him, Colin.'

He frowned. 'Saw him? Saw who?'

'Ben,' she said.

Now his blue eyes narrowed. 'Ben?'

'Ben Tremain,' she said. The name, so familiar in her head, seemed somehow alien on her tongue.

An uneasy smile appeared on his mouth. 'Dani, that's — well, it's — '

'Impossible?' she said sharply.

He nodded.

'I didn't imagine it,' she said. 'I was talking to David and when I glanced across his shoulder, there he was. I could almost have reached out and touched him.'

Colin's grip on her hand increased. 'Come on, now,' he said soothingly, as if he were trying to reassure a child who'd just had a nightmare. 'You know that couldn't be so. Perhaps it was someone who *looked* like Ben — '

'It *was* him!'

The room fell silent.

'I'm *sure* it was him,' she whispered, trying to calm her now-jangling nerves.

But deep down in her heart of hearts, she knew that it couldn't have been Ben Tremain. Because Ben Tremain *was* dead.

2

Dani got back to her neat little flat out in the suburbs just after eight o'clock that evening. She climbed out of her ice-green Metro and closed the door quietly. She felt exhausted.

With a sigh she followed the gravel drive up to the front door of the small but exclusive block of flats and let herself inside. On her doormat were an assortment of letters, but none of them were urgent or particularly important. She sifted through them, shouldering her front door shut behind her, and left them on the hall table. Tomorrow was another day; she would deal with them then.

Nothing stirred in the apartment but the ticking of clocks and the occasional whirring of the freezer. Kicking off her shoes, Dani padded into the kitchen and switched on the kettle. A cup of tea, a shower and an early night. The combination sounded good.

In the bathroom she stripped off and stepped into the shower. The hot stinging needles of water massaged the knots out of her muscles and sluiced down the firm but gentle curves of her body to puddle at her small feet. She felt the tension leaving her, and enjoyed the sensation.

Colin had been right, of course. How *could* she have seen Ben. Ben was dead — wasn't he? Or if not dead —

'Anyway, you're forgetting something,' Colin had told her just as the first tears began to escape from between her tightly-closed eyelids.

'W . . . what?' Her voice had been trembly, the voice of a lost and frightened little girl.

'If Ben *had* been at the reception, I'd have seen him,' he said. 'And I'd have recognized him straight away.' He paused. 'I didn't know him all that well, I'll grant you, but we did work together a time or two.'

24

But Dani still clung to that vision, that memory; of lively blue eyes above a straight, sharp nose and a firm, fairly sardonic mouth. His thick black hair had been swept back from his face, she remembered, and his skin had been tanned. He had lost weight, aged a little — but it was Ben. It *was*.

'There were more than three hundred people at the reception, Colin. You couldn't have noticed *all* of them.'

He considered that. 'True. But not one of those three hundred people could have gotten in without an invite, Dani. And who would have thought to send an invite to . . . ' He let the sentence die.

Die.

She switched off the water. The silence that replaced the steamy hissing was funeral. Stepping out of the shower, she caught sight of herself in the full-length mirror beside the sink. Her hair was dark and dampened by the spray. Beads of water dotted her wide shoulders and silvered her torso.

She looked at herself, *really* looked at herself, and admitted without any conceit that she could probably have married *any* man.

So why had she ended up so alone?

★ ★ ★

The following morning Dani woke early, breakfasted on toast and coffee and left for work while the leafy lane in which her flat was situated was still quiet and sleepy.

Now, as she fished her car keys from her purse, she breathed deeply of the crisp morning air, listening appreciatively to the dawn chorus issuing from the line of oaks bordering the south side of the apartments. Although she had not slept much, she felt considerably refreshed this morning, and almost ready to believe she had been mistaken about seeing Ben the previous afternoon.

She climbed into her Metro, started the engine, snapped her seat-belt shut across the front of her peach-coloured jacket and slowly edged her way out onto the road. A moment later she was coasting along the hedge-enclosed lane and on her way towards the city.

This early, the roads were still mostly empty. The sun was just beginning to creep over the hilly horizon to the east, painting the few clouds above with pink and gold. In her rear-view mirror she saw a white car some two hundred yards behind her, but paid it little attention.

When it was still trailing behind her half an hour later, however, she began to feel the first stirrings of disquiet. Her journey had taken her through the suburbs and into town. There had been a hundred or more places where the driver of the white car could have turned off, and yet he stayed doggedly behind her, almost as if he were *following* her.

Oh, she knew she was being silly, allowing her imagination to run away with her, but —

On impulse she took her next right turn, and found herself in a one-way street bordered on both sides by parked cars. She drove slowly along its length, then gasped as the white car also turned right, still keeping roughly two hundred feet behind her.

Coincidence? It could be, of course. But still she felt uneasy. She came to the end of the one-way street and turned left, onto a main road. Her heart slowed down as soon as she found herself in traffic.

Although she was beginning to feel vaguely embarrassed by her momentary panic, her large hazel eyes continued to rove up to the rear-view mirror. Her heart leapt again when she saw a white car creeping up alongside a big truck behind her. Then she released a heavy breath and a small, quirky smile touched her lips; it was a different make of car.

With an effort she concentrated on her driving. Perhaps that business yesterday afternoon had taken more out of her than she'd thought. She should take a few days off, bring forward the visit she was planning to her parents in Reading. But at the moment, with the winter collection just launched, time away from the office was a luxury she couldn't afford.

Anyway, she thought, trying to bolster her courage, why should anyone want to follow me? She wasn't a spy. She didn't have access to any world-shattering secrets . . . Just the very idea made her smile.

She glanced in her rear-view mirror again. The traffic was growing steadily now, but the mysterious white car was nowhere in sight — thank goodness.

★ ★ ★

Beau Monde operated from a large grey stone building situated about three miles from London's West End. Colin Howard rented a suite of offices on the fourth floor. Dani arrived fifteen minutes later, parked her car in the car-park behind the building and went up in the softly-lit elevator.

Because it was still quite early, Susan Keller, Beau Monde's combination receptionist and switchboard operator, was the only other member of staff already in. The pretty, fair-haired girl looked up from sorting out the morning mail and smiled pleasantly.

'Good morning, Miss McMasters.'

'Good morning, Susan. Have the papers arrived yet?'

'Yes. I've put them on your desk.'

'Thanks. Have you seen the reviews?'

'Yes — and they're great.'

Dani's smile widened in relief.

'Coffee?' the younger girl asked.

Dani nodded. 'Please.'

She left the reception behind her and pushed through a plate-glass door into a long room littered with chairs, desks, potted plants and all sorts of modern technology, from word processors to fax machines.

Three smaller rooms off to her left were separated from the main office by floor-to-ceiling partitions. A quick glance into two of the rooms told Dani that neither Colin nor Kate Allison, her assistant, had arrived yet.

She went into her own office and took off her jacket. She was wearing a matching skirt and a smart white blouse; working clothes, as opposed to the more glamorous apparel she had worn at the reception the day before. As she turned away from the coat-rack, her eyes fell to the desk for the first time.

What she saw there made a groan escape from between her lips.

On top of the newspapers Susan had set out for her sat a bunch of deep red roses, twelve in all. A dozen red roses — *the flowers Ben had always lavished upon her!*

For one giddy moment she felt weak at the knees. Before she could do anything about it, however, she heard a small sound behind her. Someone was coming out from behind the open office door — someone who had been *hiding* there!

She turned, alarm mingling with her sense of shock and anger. She saw a tall man standing directly in front of her, but in her momentary confusion she failed to recognize him.

He said, 'Surprise!'

She took a pace back. 'Uh . . . What — ?'

Suddenly his features swam into sharp focus. She became aware of his remarkably green eyes first, then his long, straight nose and the wide, appealing smile revealed beneath it. His shoulder-length salt-and-pepper hair, his clear, tanned skin —

At last recognition dawned.

'David!'

David Mason, the most popular and gifted of all her designers, allowed a frown to replace his beaming smile. 'I'm sorry if I startled you,' he said with concern.

With a supreme effort she recovered herself, running one hand up through her short, butter-coloured hair. 'It's all right, David, it's . . . it's my fault. I was miles aw — '

'No, I should have thought. You obviously haven't quite got over that turn you had yesterday. It was stupid of me.'

She went around the desk and sat down. Her nerves had been badly rattled, but she would soon get over that. 'Are these from you?' she asked, indicating the flowers in a way that suggested she were reluctant to touch them.

'Just my way of thanking you for all your help and encouragement,' he replied, obviously annoyed with himself. 'This deal with De Sala in France is entirely down to you, you know.'

'Well, I wouldn't go *that* far.'

'It's true. If you hadn't come along when you did, I'd still be posing for a bunch of amateur artists who couldn't tell one end of a pencil from the other!' His jade-coloured eyes grew serious. 'I really mean it, Dani. I owe you practically everything.'

There was a light rap at the door and

Susan Keller brought Dani's coffee in. David offered her a sour smile. 'My little surprise backfired, I'm afraid,' he confessed.

Susan smiled up at him. 'I told you it was a bad idea,' she replied. 'I'm sorry, Miss McMasters — I should have warned you that there was a maniac in here waiting to pounce on you.'

'Never mind, I forgive you.' Dani switched her gaze back to David, who was still standing there with his hands thrust into the pockets of his padded denim jacket, looking sheepish. 'Thank you for the roses. They're beautiful.' She picked them up and ran her eyes across their delicate crimson petals. It had been such a long time since anyone had bought her flowers . . .

'Would you like me to put them in water for you, Miss McMasters?'

'If you wouldn't mind, Susan.'

Dani took a small white envelope from between the stems and handed the roses to the girl, who then left the room in search of a vase. Opening the envelope, Dani read the short message scribbled on the card inside. DANI — THANKS A BUNCH! DAVID.

She looked up again. 'Have you seen the reviews?'

'Some.'

'And?'

'They all seem to agree — this season's collection is among your best so far.'

'I had little to do with it,' she replied, skimming down each of the fashion columns with a growing smile. 'Here, you see! Mason, Mason, Mason . . .' Her laugh was musical. 'They're all raving about *you*, David — just as I knew they would!'

He shrugged modestly. 'Hey, but listen . . . How do you *really* feel now? You gave us all the most awful shock yesterday, just fainting the way you did.'

She glanced away from him. 'I'm fine. Really.'

'You still look a little pale.'

'I feel great, I promise.'

The sound of voices drifted in to

them from the outer office, where the rest of the staff were finally beginning to show up. Taking that as his cue to leave, David checked his wrist-watch. 'Well, don't let me detain you. I'm only here to go over the preliminary sub-licensing agreements with Colin, but — have you got anything planned for lunch?'

Dani considered. 'I don't think so. There's a couple of design school students I promised to see at eleven, but I should be through by, say, one o'clock.'

'I'll meet you here then, if you like. We can eat at that little Italian place just across the road.'

She nodded. 'I'd like that.'

After he was gone she read his note again, and smiled. He really was the most likeable of men. But then she remembered the roses, and her thoughts returned to Ben . . .

Just six years ago, she thought. And yet it might just as well have been a lifetime. So much had changed. Her life today was entirely different to the life she'd known then.

She'd first met Ben Tremain amid the rolling greenery of Gasgoigne House, in Nottinghamshire. His reputation as a fashion photographer was already gaining momentum; that's why Colin Howard had chosen him to create the very first Beau Monde catalogue.

Dani had been just one of several models hired for the seven-day shoot. She had come to modelling relatively late, having first established that, though she might be extremely artistic, art school was not really for her. A High Street chain-store with a strong line in fashion had taken her on as a sales assistant, but the work had been boring and without challenge. It was whilst discussing her growing discontent one Friday lunchtime that a colleague had suggested she become a model.

'Lord knows, you've certainly got the face and figure for it. Combine that with your love of good fashion and it sounds to me as if you've found the perfect occupation.'

At first Dani wasn't sure. She'd done some posing at art school, and found it surprisingly painless, but . . .

It had taken her six more months to finally make up her mind to give it a go. Her parents, bless them, had been behind her all the way. She promptly set about compiling a portfolio and registered with a modelling agency.

A few small jobs had followed. The Beau Monde shoot at Nottinghamshire, however, was her first big assignment, and on the morning she arrived, she had been a very nervous twenty-year-old indeed.

She remembered that first meeting with Colin so clearly. Although it had yet to establish itself as a major fashion store, Beau Monde was already attracting more and more attention. That was why Colin and wife Sandra had decided to go ahead and commission a catalogue featuring their various ranges.

Dani still recalled how Colin had fussed around the girls like a mother hen, making sure that his dressers, make-up artists and hair stylists had all done their jobs to the best of their considerable abilities.

With butterflies in her tummy, Dani had stood there on the fringes of all the chaos, watching the professionals at work for what was virtually the very first time. It had been a beautiful day, she remembered, June; and the sky was a breathtaking blue bowl overhead, the sun a perfect, glowing orb.

The first time she saw Ben Tremain, he had been standing amid a veritable forest of tripods and arc lamps. She had been struck not so much by his height — a generous six feet one — or his undoubted good-looks, but more by his sober, almost grim manner. She had heard that when he worked he did so with a commitment and pace that bordered on the obsessive. He had certainly been involved that day, giving orders for a light to be tilted this way or that and calling for one of his two assistants to fetch a certain lens or filter.

Dani had become fascinated by his professionalism. He seemed to know exactly the atmosphere he wanted to convey in any given picture, and made the people around him share that vision by his use of words and the quick, expressive gestures of his long-fingered hands.

Gradually she had found herself studying his face. He was somewhere in his middle-twenties, with a long, lean face, evenly-spaced eyes the same dusty blue as a robin's egg and a long, straight nose with flared nostrils. His squarish jaw was pitted by a shallow dimple and blued by a faint shadow of stubble. His mouth was sober and unsmiling, his lips the very palest of pinks. Sunlight made the thick black hair sweeping back from his seamed forehead appear midnight-blue in places. His plain white shirt, darkened here and there with perspiration, had been partially unbuttoned to reveal a bronzed chest, not muscular exactly, but tight and compact, across which lay a light dusting of hair. His legs, encased in tight bleached jeans, were long, and his manner, though distant, was brisk and efficient.

'All right . . . Danielle, isn't it? You're next.'

Dani came out of her reverie to find Colin looking at her over the clipboard he held in his hands. He'd looked hot and bothered there in his lightweight safari suit and sky-blue shirt, still so formal and harassed despite the pleasantly casual atmosphere of camaraderie surrounding the location.

Dani had experienced a fleeting instant of panic. This was it, then; the moment she had been both longing for and dreading. Nodding, she had weaved through all the tripods and camera cases, careful not to trip over the cables snaking this way and that across the gravel and grass. Gasgoigne House loomed up behind her, stately and regal, its red bricks and white Georgian window-frames touched by the warm sun above.

Taking a series of nerve-settling deep breaths, Dani went straight up to Ben, who was rewinding the film in the camera around his neck, and said, 'Good afternoon, Mr Tremain.'

He had barely glanced in her direction. 'Just stand over there. I'll be with you in a minute.'

Immediately she had bristled. He was obviously not going to be among the most pleasant men with whom she had ever worked. Turning on her heel, she had walked over to the spot he had indicated, a narrow gravel path bordered by neatly-trimmed grass dotted with buttercups, and waited for her dark eyes to adjust to the glare of the arcs.

Suddenly a voice had come out of the wall of light in front of her. 'Is there something wrong?'

She shook her head. 'No. Why?'

'You're frowning.'

'I'm sorry, I didn't mean to. I was just — '

'Yes, yes, all right. Just try to relax. Look a little to your right. That's it. Try to imagine that you're waiting for someone. A lover or something. Show me a hint of impatience tinged with anticipation.'

She brushed imaginary creases from the front of the sequined and beaded black knitted dress she was wearing. It was a superb design, with padded shoulders and two intricate designs sloping down across the front, one in gold, one in red. But it was the wrong kind of dress to have to model on so warm a day.

Ben straightened up from behind a tripod-mounted camera and quickly glanced around, obviously exasperated by something. 'Can somebody come and wipe her brow? I've got the sun bouncing right off her forehead!'

An assistant hurried over and dabbed carefully at her face with a tissue. She stood there patiently, trying to ignore the sinking sensation in her stomach. It was all going wrong, she thought miserably. She was not only *slowing* everyone down, she was *letting* them down as well.

'That's better,' Ben muttered as his assistant moved out of the way. Again he told Dani to imagine she were waiting for someone, to register a sense of anticipation. She tried to blank her mind of all distractions and concentrate on the job at hand, but evidently she didn't succeed. 'I said imagine you're waiting for your *lover*,' he snapped five minutes later, 'not a number ten bus!'

Her small hands clenched into angry fists at her sides. 'I'm trying my best!'

'Well, perhaps you ought to try a little harder!'

She felt her lips thinning down to a narrow line. Everyone was watching her. She thought she heard a few of the other girls begin to giggle, and her normally even temper slipped.

'Are you always this rude to people?'

she asked almost before she realized she had spoken. 'Or are you just making an exception for me?'

He came around the tripod and strode across to her, his own lean face tight with anger. 'It's not a case of being rude,' he retorted. 'It's more a case of one professional trying to work with another!'

A tingle of outrage washed across her face. 'Are you calling me unprofessional?' she asked indignantly.

A sardonic smile twisted his lips. 'If the cap fits . . . '

'How *dare* you! I — '

He interrupted whatever she was going to say next, which, in retrospect, was probably just as well. 'Look, are you going to give me the look I want, or are you going to make way for someone else who *can*?'

'*I'll* do it!' she said with determination.

And she had, too — eventually. But when at last it was all over, the humiliation of his treatment made her leave the set at a run, with tears silvering her cheeks and her dreams of a modelling career shattered almost beyond repair.

3

Colin Howard had hurried after her, still clutching his clipboard. His ruddy face showed his concern; his dark blue eyes mirrored his discomfort.

'Danielle? It *is* Danielle, isn't it?' He glanced down at the clipboard. 'Yes . . . Danielle, *please*, not so fast! This isn't a race, you know!'

But it was, at least as far as Dani was concerned; a race to get to one of the two caravans set up on the edge of the field surrounding the estate, a race to change back into her own clothes and hurry back home to Reading.

'Danielle, please — oops!'

The sounds he made slipping a little on the grass made her pause and turn at last, just to make certain he was all right.

Righting himself before he could lose balance completely, he offered her a sheepish smile as his scrubbed face coloured even more. 'My goodness, that was close!' he said in mock relief. 'I must be getting too old for all this chasing after pretty young girls!'

The faint beginnings of a smile touched her quivery lips as she went back to join him. About a hundred yards away Ben Tremain was watching them with his hands on his hips while his assistants started to move all their equipment to a new location.

'Are you all right?' she asked quietly.

Colin nodded, breathing hard. 'I am now that I've made you smile again,' he replied. 'There . . . that's better. Now; may I *walk* you back to the caravan, ma'am? That seems like a far more civilized notion than trying to break the four-minute mile!'

She dipped her blonde head as her smile widened. 'All right. Thank you.' They began walking side by side. 'I'm sorry,' she said at last, her voice softened by embarrassment. 'About letting everyone down just now.'

'I wasn't aware that you had. But I think we'll get over it, don't you?'

She made no reply.

'If it's any consolation, I thought you had just the right look of anticipation,' he said kindly. 'As far as I was concerned, Ben Tremain was talking nonsense.'

Dani looked over at his profile, pleased to find an ally. 'Really?'

Colin nodded. 'Oh, yes.' His grin broadened. 'The number ten bus doesn't run past Gasgoigne House.'

She studied him for a moment more, then felt the last of the tension leave her. He chuckled at his own joke and she joined in, punching him lightly on the arm as she made some good-natured remark about his cheek.

And that was the day their friendship began.

★ ★ ★

By the time she was ready to leave the beautiful stately home in

Nottinghamshire, Dani no longer felt like catching a train all the way back to Reading. She had calmed down now, thanks to Colin, and was able to reflect upon her first day before the cameras without becoming too upset.

All right — so Tremain had been tough on her, far more so than he'd been with any of the other girls. But maybe it had just *seemed* that way because Dani had not yet been around the business long enough to know otherwise. The more she thought about it, the more she became convinced that this was indeed the case.

When she finally rose from the table in front of one of the brightly-lit mirrors and slipped her bag over her shoulder, she felt much, much better about the entire affair. Leaving the caravan, she saw the other models and various assistants trooping back across the field in her direction and glanced at her watch. It was four-thirty already; the end of the first day's shoot.

Her initial reaction was to avoid them

all; Lord alone knew what they must have thought of her. But then she realized that she would have to see them again at some stage. She might as well get it over and done with.

As she set out to meet them she noticed that Ben Tremain was not among them. Thank goodness. A few of the girls waved to her. One or two asked if she were feeling better. Colin Howard, still behaving like a mother hen, caught her eye and asked quietly, 'Will we be seeing you again tomorrow, Dani?'

And Dani had replied with a firm nod. 'If you'll still have me — yes.'

★   ★   ★

For convenience, Colin had booked them all in at the combination pub and guest-house in the village six miles from Gasgoigne House. That evening, while some of the girls went out for a walk along the peaceful, winding streets and a few of the others occupied themselves with card-games, TV or just socializing over drinks, Dani went into the olde worlde dining-room and found a secluded corner table from which she ordered a chicken salad and an ice-cold orange-juice.

The only other diners were an elderly couple on the other side of the room, conversing in low voices between mouthfuls of salmon and lettuce. Dani studied them for a moment, envying them their easy companionship. For them life was settled and orderly. For her — as she was now starting to realize — it was only just beginning, and full of uncertainty.

She was just finishing her meal when a shadow fell across her table. Looking up, she saw with surprise that Ben Tremain was standing over her.

'Oh — !'

His grim face made an attempt to relax, but his smile was brief and uncertain. 'I'm sorry if I'm disturbing you . . . I'll come back later, if you like.'

She was at once both puzzled and

apprehensive. Colin Howard had been only too happy that she had decided to stay on for the entire week's shoot. But supposing this raven-headed photographer didn't care to work with her any more? What if he had come to tell her that she should leave after all?

Keeping her concern well-hidden, she gestured to the empty chair on the other side of the table. 'No, please; sit down.'

'Thanks. What I've got to say won't take long, anyway.'

That sounded ominous, she thought. Setting her cutlery down, she pushed her plate aside. She hadn't had much appetite to begin with; now it had disappeared completely.

When he said nothing more, however, she felt compelled to break the silence between them. 'Look, I really *am* terribly sorry about this af — '

'No, no, it wasn't your fault. That's why I'm here; to apologize to *you*. I had no idea this was your first assignment. That's why I suppose I just expected you to give me the look I wanted without any bother.' This time his smile stayed longer on his lips. 'When Mr Howard explained it all to me I felt awful.' He eyed her closely, his lean face bathed in the golden, sinking sunlight that spilled in through the nearby window, and something of amusement appeared in his depthless blue eyes. 'You weren't *too* upset, were you?'

She forced a smile, relieved that he hadn't come to give her her marching orders after all. 'No, not after Colin — Mr Howard — calmed me down.'

'I'm glad. I take it you haven't had much experience in front of the cameras, then?'

'I've had some.'

'Well, there's more to it than modelling for a bunch of amateurs every other Tuesday evening — as I believe you found out today.'

'I know *that*,' she replied, irritated by his implication that her experience had been limited to amateur photography clubs.

'It's not just a case of looking this way or that,' he went on. 'You've got to build up a relationship between yourself and the camera. You've got to *love* it. Love *it*, and it will love *you*.'

She nodded. 'I suppose I *was* a bit self-conscious this afternoon.'

He chuckled. '*I'll* say!'

Again his vague air of condescension irritated her. 'I was trying my best,' she said sharply.

At last he seemed to realize that he ought to be a bit more diplomatic. 'I'm sure you'll do better tomorrow.'

'I hope so. I'll certainly remember what you said about falling in love with the camera.'

Suddenly an idea occurred to him. 'Have you finished your meal?'

'Yes.'

'Have you got anything else planned for tonight? I know some of the others have congregated in the bar — '

'No, no, I was just going to go for a walk, that's all.'

'All right.' He stood up. 'I'll meet you

outside in ten minutes.' And without waiting to hear what *she* might have to say about it, he hurried from the room.

Dani frowned, wondering what he had in mind. A moment later she, too, stood up and went through the oak-panelled reception, into the car-park outside.

The evening air was pleasantly peaceful, and now that it was beginning to cool off she wondered if she should quickly go up to her room and grab a cardigan to complement her sleeveless white blouse and pleated lemon skirt.

Before she could decide, Ben appeared at the guest-house entrance, a black case held in his left hand. 'Ah, there you are!' Away from the pressures of his work he seemed much more relaxed, not at all the ogre with whom she had traded harsh words that afternoon. He came over to her wearing the most appealing smile, took her arm and steered her in the direction of his car, a smart-looking wine-red Mercedes sports car.

'Where are we going?' she asked, not quite sure if she entirely approved of being urged along in such a way.

'Not far,' he replied vaguely. He dug a ring of keys from his jeans pocket and unlocked, then opened, the passenger door for her. 'A couple of miles.'

She paused before climbing into the car, now almost comically suspicious of his motives. 'Why?'

His grin chased some of the lines from his forehead. 'It's all right; I'm not going to eat you up, if that's what's worrying you.'

He strode around the front of the car and unlocked his own door. Soon they were both settled inside the car, and he was reversing out of his parking-space, then steering them out onto the narrow main road.

When they were speeding through the picturesque little village, Dani began to grow aware of his aftershave. It smelled of citrus fruits, and she found it alarmingly intoxicating. 'Have you, ah . . . have you done many fashion catalogues like the one you're doing at the moment?' she asked awkwardly.

He nodded, keeping his now-lively blue eyes on the hedge-bordered road ahead. 'A few. I've always enjoyed good fashion, the challenge of trying to bring out the texture of the fabrics and the quality of the models. It's something you can't always achieve when you're doing magazine spreads. You haven't got the time, for one thing. But with a catalogue, well, it's different. For once, the client shares your desire to get the best possible results.'

Off to Dani's left the hedge began to break away to reveal a field. In the field stood a windmill which had now fallen into disuse and disrepair. Setting sunlight outlined the building with a strong golden penumbra, mixing perfectly with the greens and whites and reds already on show. The effect was breathtaking.

He seemed to read her thoughts. 'Yes, it's stunning, isn't it?'

'Do you know this part of the country well?'

'Fairly. My family originally came from Long Eaton, which is only about fifteen miles away. We lived there until I was eleven, when my dad's job meant that we had to move down south. I've never forgotten those early years up here, though. I was very fortunate to have countryside like this as my back garden.'

Dani slowly felt herself beginning to warm to him at last. No longer did he appear arrogant or condescending. Now he was relaxed, and his deep, cultured voice held a quality that relaxed *her* too. Still, she wondered where he was taking her — and for what purpose.

Fifteen minutes later they turned off the twisting country road and followed a rutted track deeper into the surrounding countryside. Grass grew tall to either side of them, and trees began to scratch at the sky, screening them from any passing traffic. Dani tried to check her watch without letting him see. The time was almost seven-fifteen.

Why could he possibly be bringing her to this lonely spot? She felt her tummy give an unpleasant flutter.

Suddenly he braked, and switched off the engine. Silence settled over them like a shroud.

She swallowed softly. 'Are we . . . here?' she asked.

He smiled at her. 'Yes, we're here. Come on.'

They got out of the car. Dani saw that he had brought them to an isolated spot full of long grass, wild flowers and trees. About thirty feet directly ahead of them a stream chuckled past, and reeds grew tall along its gently-sloping banks. Insects buzzed through the air; here and there she spotted fluttering butterflies adding brighter colours to all the greens and browns.

'What a lovely place,' she breathed. She still wasn't certain of his motives, however, and that stopped her from appreciating all the wild beauty even more.

'Yes it is,' he agreed. 'You could trace that stream all the way up to the River Smilie, if you wanted to.' He reached into the car and brought out the black case he'd fetched with him. Dani eyed it cautiously.

'Now,' he said, opening the case. 'To business.'

Dani knew a moment of near-panic. What did the case contain? Rope? A knife? A gun?

Then he brought out an expensive-looking 35mm camera, which he hung around his neck, and she almost sagged with relief.

'The one way to stop you feeling self-conscious in front of a camera,' he explained quite pleasantly, 'is to get you used to it. That's what we're going to do now.'

Dani felt her cheeks flush. 'Oh, well, I don't — '

The camera clicked. 'I think I'll call that one 'Indecision',' he pronounced, grinning broadly.

She could hardly believe that such a change could come over this man who had stood so grim and distant all afternoon. She smiled and he took another picture.

'Hmm. Didn't quite get the focus right on that one,' he said half to himself. 'Never mind. We'll call it 'Through the Mist'.'

'You *do* know that you're wasting your film, don't you?' she said.

'I've got plenty of film to waste.'

'Not to mention your time.'

'I'm not wasting my time, believe me.'

He took another picture.

And that was almost exactly how they spent the next hour, until it grew too dark to take more pictures. His gentle, amiable voice gradually put her at ease, and slowly she began to forget that the camera was there. Under his gentle coaxing her confidence grew, surprising no-one more than herself, until at length he reached the end of his second roll of film and put the camera away.

'I *knew* you had it in you,' he said with a laugh. 'I'm seldom wrong when it comes to spotting that special something some people have about them.'

His praise both pleased and embarrassed her. 'Star quality, you mean?' she asked, teasing him.

'No, I mean it — *really*.' He closed the case and placed it on the narrow back seat, then glanced up at the darkening sky. 'Hmm. Looks as if I've kept you out longer than intended. Never mind — it won't take us long to get back.'

He hurried around the car to open the door for her, a gesture that altered her initial impression of him even more. For a moment they faced each other in the gloom. They might have been the only two people left on earth. It was an intimate moment, and made her feel light-headed.

Then she climbed into the car and he hurried around the front. Twenty minutes later they were back at the guest-house, and Dani was floating on air.

* * *

'Where shall I put the flowers, Miss McMasters?'

Dani blinked a few times as she came back out of the past. Susan Keller was standing in her office doorway, the dozen red roses David Mason had bought for her arranged in a pale grey vase.

Dani indicated the low shelf on the wall to her left. 'Just on the end there, please. Thanks.'

She opened a folder and sifted through some papers. There were a few material orders to chase up today, in addition to all her usual duties, but glancing at her watch, Dani saw that it was still too early to start phoning around.

A light rapping at the door made her look up. Colin Howard was peering in at her, his scrubbed red face expectant. 'Hi! I won't keep you a minute. I just wondered how the patient was doing this morning.'

She frowned. 'Patient?'

'Yes — *you*.'

'Oh, fine.'

'Good.'

He came into the room and sat down in the visitor's chair on the other side of the desk. 'To be honest, I'm surprised to see you. I *did* tell you to take a couple of days off.'

'Yes, I know, but I feel fine.'

He arched an eyebrow. 'Really?'

'Well, I don't feel *ill*, let's put it that way.'

He glanced over at the flowers. 'Secret admirer?'

'David,' she replied. 'He should be around here somewhere.'

'Yes, I'm supposed to be seeing him this morning.' He rose and brushed down the jacket of his silver-grey suit. 'Well, no rest for the wicked.'

'No.'

He studied her with concern. 'Dani, about yesterday — '

'It's all right, Colin. I thought I saw Ben, but I know now that I couldn't have.' A sour smile touched her full lips. 'I'm not losing my mind or heading for a nervous breakdown, I promise you. It was just a case of mistaken identity.'

He nodded. 'Well, if you change your mind and decide that you *do* feel like a break — '

Her phone began to ring, and her smile grew more good-natured. 'Chance would be a fine thing.' Then she picked up the receiver. 'Hello, Danielle McMasters. Can I help you?'

*   *   *

The memory of that first encounter with Ben stayed with Dani for the rest of the day, right through a seemingly endless round of phone calls, her eleven o'clock meeting with the design school students, lunch with David Mason and on into the afternoon. The roses on the shelf were a constant reminder of that happier time.

Ben had taught her more about her chosen profession in that one evening than anyone else could have done in a lifetime. But the euphoria she'd known the night he'd driven her to the chuckling stream and then brought her back safe and sound soon wore off; the very next day he was back to his grim and distant self, his concentration focused entirely on the job at hand.

Dani remembered the hurt she'd felt when her beaming smile was returned with a curt nod. As far as he seemed concerned, the previous evening might never have happened.

With an effort she had shaken off her sense of disappointment. She should have known better than to assume Ben's interest in her had been anything more than professional. As much as it hurt to do so, she resolved to put it down to experience and get on with her life.

She did, too. After the Beau Monde

shoot she went on to other jobs, even a television commercial. In the next six weeks she spent so much time away from home that she decided it would probably be more convenient for all concerned if she found herself a flat in London and used that as her base.

Two months after the Beau Monde shoot a large cardboard envelope with the initials 'B.T.P.' stamped across the top left-hand corner was delivered to Dani's new address. It had been forwarded on by the agency for whom she worked. With a puzzled frown she had opened the envelope and reached inside.

Her gasp had been full of surprise as she drew out a thin stack of glossy 10 × 8 pictures — the very pictures Ben had taken of her that beautiful summer's evening!

Quickly she went through the photographs. Here was the one he'd called 'Indecision', there the blurry one he'd jokingly christened 'Through the Mist'. At once she felt a great sense of pride well up inside her, because under Ben's tutelage she really *had* been able to express all those emotions he'd so wanted to capture; happiness, sorrow, joy, melancholy, sensuality, anticipation, wistfulness —

But she was even more touched by the knowledge that he hadn't forgotten all about that wonderful evening after all. He'd remembered. He'd remembered *her*.

Suddenly her hazel eyes came to the compliments slip he had put in with the pictures. Ben Tremain Photographic. She checked the address. His studio was based in London — no more than a ten-minute drive away!

She knew she must phone him, to thank him for the pictures, but just the thought of talking to him again made her heart beat faster. Teasingly she reminded herself that she was supposed to be a sophisticated, mature girl-about-town now, not some giggling adolescent. But although she'd had a couple of boyfriends in the past, none had affected her as profoundly as Ben.

She studied the compliments slip again. As nervous as she felt about calling him, she could hardly wait. Going over to the phone on the hall table, she dialled the number and listened to the ringing at the other end with a fluttering tummy.

At last there was a click in her ear. A voice said, 'Hello, Ben Tremain Photographic.'

For one awful moment she didn't think she was going to be able to talk around the lump in her throat. Then she managed to croak, 'Oh, hello. Is Mr Tremain there, please?'

'Speaking.'

Her stomach gave another lurch. 'Oh, ah . . . hello there. This is Danielle McMasters.'

She thought there might be a pause while he placed the name, but to her secret delight he remembered her straight away. 'Dani! Hi! You got the pictures, I take it?'

'Yes. That's why I'm calling. They're

wonderful. I'm terribly proud of them.'

'You should be. I told you you had it in you. Have you seen the Beau Monde catalogue yet?'

'No, not yet.'

'I had a couple of copies through the post yesterday. As immodest as it may sound, I have a feeling you'll be pleased with your work *there*, too.'

There was so much she wanted to say, but now that it had come to it, she didn't really know where to start. Instead she said rather lamely, 'Well . . . how have you been keeping?'

'Busy.'

'Oh, I'll go if — '

'Nonsense. I'm never too busy to speak to a talented young model — although I *will* own up to having been wrist-deep in developer and fixative when you rang.'

She wasn't sure if he were joking or serious. 'No, no, I'll go. But — '

'Yes?'

'Well . . . those pictures . . . it really was most kind of you to remember me

71

and send them . . . I wonder . . . ' She knew it was probably a mistake to ask, that she might only be setting herself up for another fall, but she really *was* taken by his kindness, and wanted to repay it. 'Could I buy you lunch, perhaps?'

There was a pause at the other end of the line, and she realized with a sinking feeling that she *had* been wrong to take the initiative and ask him out.

But then he said, 'Why, sure — if you *want* to. But there's really no need.'

Her heart was fairly hammering now. 'It's the least I can do. Do you have any preference?'

He told her that there was a rather good Cantonese restaurant not far from his studio, and that, yes, he'd be free at twelve-thirty. Appreciative of the invite, and mindful of what must, at the moment, be quite a modest income, he tactfully chose not to mention that the restaurant's prices were very reasonable.

'I'll see you at twelve-thirty, then,' she said brightly.

His voice held a smile. 'Look forward to it.'

As she rang off, Dani felt happier in herself than she had for some time, and the realization surprised her. It was all too easy to fall into a routine, she supposed, to get up every morning, go to work, come home and go back to bed. Her lunch date with Ben Tremain was something out of the ordinary, and even just the prospect of it was already adding a sparkle to her day.

But there was more to it than that. That she felt some attraction to the photographer was undeniable. Not only was he good-looking; she also sensed that there was a warm and gentle nature trying to get out from beneath the sober and distracted mantle he wore when working.

She had just entered her bedroom, and was about to sort through her clothes to find the nicest outfit to wear, when there was a knock at the door. Frowning — for today was a rest day and she'd been expecting no visitors

— she went to answer it.

The postman was standing on her doorstep. 'Sorry to bother you again,' he said, proffering a white envelope. 'I had another letter for you, but the idiots down at the sorting-office put it in the wrong place in my pile.'

Dani took the envelope with a smile. 'That's all right. It got here in the end.'

She closed the door and looked at the envelope. This, too, had 'B.T.P.' stamped on the top left-hand corner, and it had also been forwarded on to her by the modelling agency.

Curiously Dani tore open the envelope and withdrew two folded sheets from inside. Opening them out, she saw that the top copy was an invoice from Ben's studio.

'*To supply 28 b/w prints on 10 × 8 glossy stock as per attached schedule — £85.00.*'

Dani was dumbstruck. She had to read the details one more time before they sank in.

Kindness my eye! she thought indignantly. Ben Tremain hadn't sent her the pictures as a memento of that very special evening. He'd done it purely as a job of work! And . . . she crumpled the invoice between her small fists, beginning to tremble now with anger and humiliation.

And not content with charging her the most exorbitant price for the photos — he was going to let her buy him lunch as well!

4

Dani drummed her fingertips impatiently on the dragon and weeping willow-embroidered tablecloth. It was twelve-forty and Ben still hadn't shown up at the restaurant. An Oriental waiter came over and asked if she would care to order yet. She shook her head, still so angry — with herself as much as Ben — that she didn't trust herself to speak.

Sensing her mood, the waiter wisely left her alone.

She blamed herself for the misunderstanding. After all, Ben had a business to run, and overheads were high. She'd had no right to assume that the pictures were a gift.

But Ben was in the wrong, too. He should not have presumed to print up the photographs and then charge her for them without first checking that she really did want them. And worse than that, he should not have allowed her to add insult to injury by accepting her invitation to lunch. He was only interested in money, after all, not *her* —

The restaurant door opened with a barely audible creak and she looked up sharply. Ben stood there, looking around. When at last he spotted her, a broad smile lit up his long face and he waved the *maître d'* away, weaving between the other tables to reach her.

Despite her anger, she could not ignore the tingling in her tummy just at the sight of him. Although she hadn't seen him since the Beau Monde shoot, he looked exactly as she remembered him, tall, slim, raven-headed and distinguished. He wore a black jacket over an open-necked white shirt and smart designer jeans. His square jaw was still blued by a faint sketching of stubble, and he still smelled intoxicatingly of citrus fruits. He looked pleased to see her; his smile was an ivory flash, and his blue eyes reflected a warm, inner pleasure. But she was not about to allow herself to be swayed by his undoubted charm.

'Danielle! I'm sorry I'm a bit late — '

Much to his surprise, she stood up as soon as he sat down.

'Oh, don't worry about that, *Mr* Tremain,' she said formally. '*I'm* sorry. Because I've got another engagement. Yes, it was silly of me to forget, wasn't it? But don't worry — I've got time to pay my debts.'

He looked at her as if she might be mad. 'I'm sorry? I don't — '

'Here,' she said, thrusting an envelope at him in such a way that he could not help but take it. 'I think you'll find that this settles the account.'

And so saying, she swept around the table and strode purposefully towards the exit.

Behind her, Ben swivelled around in his chair, frowning and with his mouth open in surprise, 'Dani?'

When he realized she wasn't going to turn around again, he fairly leapt up and hurried after her, uncomfortably aware of the strange looks he was receiving from the Cantonese staff. 'Dani! Hey, just wait up a moment! What's the matter?'

They were out on the street before she spun on her heel so suddenly that he nearly ran into her. 'There's nothing the matter,' she snapped in reply. 'Nothing at all — now.'

'But — '

She turned away again and continued up the street.

'Oh, for heaven's sake, woman!'

She threw a disparaging look over her shoulder. 'Just leave me alone!'

Standing there on the pavement outside the restaurant, with the staff now flattening their noses at the window to make sure they didn't miss anything more of the one-sided disagreement, Ben switched his attention to the envelope in his hand. He opened it quickly and took out a cheque made payable to his studio.

'What in heaven's name . . . ?'

His voice trailed off. He glanced first

at the grinning Cantonese inside the restaurant, then back along the street. But by then it was too late. Dani was nowhere in sight.

* * *

When Dani got back to her flat, the telephone was ringing.

Hurrying through the door, she snatched up the receiver. 'Yes, hello?'

'Dani, it's Cheryl.'

Cheryl was one of the girls down at the modelling agency. Unbuttoning her jacket, Dani leaned against the wall and closed her eyes. She was still wound-up from her brief meeting with Ben, but tried to keep that out of her voice. 'Hi, Cheryl. What can I do for you?'

'Well, it's more a case of what *I* can do for *you* — I think.'

Dani frowned. 'I'm sorry, but I'm not in the mood for conundrums today. You'd better just say whatever it is in plain English.'

At the other end of the line Cheryl

laughed. 'Fair enough. I've just had Ben Tremain on the phone. You remember him — he's the guy who did that Beau M — '

'Yes, I remember.'

Cheryl obviously failed to hear the slight edge that had crept into Dani's voice. 'Well, evidently he remembers *you*,' she went on. 'He just rang to see if we could give him your address.'

'Don't.'

'Well, obviously we wouldn't without your permission. That's why I was calling.'

'I don't want him to know anything about me, Cheryl.'

'Oh, it's like *that*, is it?'

'Like *what*?'

'I had no idea you two knew each other well enough to have had a lover's tiff.'

'We *don't*!'

'All right, all right. If you say so.'

'I do.'

'I won't give out any details, then.'

Dani nodded absently, her eyes

81

roving across the pictures she'd left scattered across the table, beside the phone. 'Thanks.'

She put the phone down and looked around the silent flat. She had been so happy just a few short hours ago. Now she felt restless, and annoyed — with the world in general and herself in particular.

On impulse she decided to go out. It was a glorious August day, warm but with a refreshing breeze. Regent's Park might be nice. Just a stroll, perhaps a relaxing half-hour beside the lake, feeding the ducks.

The phone started ringing again while she was in the kitchen, getting some bread ready for her visit to the lake. Suppressing a sigh, she went into the hallway to answer it.

'Hello?'

Cheryl said, 'I don't think Mr Tremain is very happy with you at the moment, my girl.'

Dani, already touchy, bristled even more. 'To be perfectly honest, Cheryl, I don't give a fig.'

She heard a shrug in the other girl's voice. 'Well, if you're sure . . . '

'I am.'

'All right. But he asked me to give you a message. He said, 'What am I supposed to have done wrong?' There was something else about a cheque, but I didn't really understand that.'

'It's all right. He was just raving. He does that, so I've been told. Just goes off on a tangent for no apparent reason.'

'Sounds to me as if you're better off without him, then.'

'I'm sure I am,' Dani said in a hollow voice. 'Bye.'

★   ★   ★

As she had expected, the park was glorious beneath the fine August sunshine, and dotted with all manner of visitors. The many benches and flat green fields beckoned to families and workers on late lunchbreaks alike. Dani found a spot beside the lake that was shaded by thick-boled trees and threw bread to the ducks. Before long she was almost surrounded by a whole skein of the aquatic birds, all of them calling for more tidbits.

Much later she toyed with the idea of visiting the nearby zoo. It had been a long time since she'd done anything so impulsive. But time was marching on, and she decided reluctantly that she'd better head for home if she wanted to miss the rush-hour.

No sooner had she arrived back at her flat than there was a ringing at the door. Leaving her jacket and bag on a chair in the living-room, Dani went to see who it was.

A middle-aged lady stood in the hallway wearing a brown smock embroidered with the logo of a popular home-delivery florist. In her hands was a bunch of twelve deep-red roses, which she offered to Dani with a smile.

'For you,' she said.

The woman gave Dani no time to

think about the identity of the sender. Only when the front door was closed again did she allow curiosity to replace her surprise.

Back in the living-room she unwrapped the blooms and opened the tiny envelope which had been slipped in among them.

'*Hmmm!*' she breathed as soon as her hazel eyes read the name at the bottom of the short message. ''*Dani; if I've done something wrong, I'm sorry. Why don't you give me a call and tell me what it is? Ben.*''

The nerve of the man! The nerve of *Cheryl*, giving out her address when she'd specifically asked that it remain confidential!

Still . . . there was no denying that the flowers were beautiful. Dani eyed them thoughtfully. Could it be that Ben really *didn't* know what he'd done wrong? Come to that, had he really done *anything* that was so terrible?

She took the flowers through to the kitchen and found a vase in the cupboard beneath the sink. Maybe she'd over-reacted a little. After all, nobody had *forced* her to ask Ben to lunch. He had probably decided to accept more out of good manners than anything else.

She began to feel a little foolish.

When the phone rang twenty minutes later, she thought seriously about having it disconnected. Then again, perhaps she should invest in a telephone answering machine —

'Yes, hello?'

There was a pause. Then Ben's voice came softly into her ear. 'I *was* going to wait until you called *me*,' he said in that deep, relaxing way he had. 'But then I got to thinking that maybe you wouldn't bother. So I decided to take the initiative.'

Dani drew in a deep breath to calm her racing pulse. 'Who gave you this number?' she asked, trying to sound indignant. 'How did you find out my address?'

'Directory Enquiries,' he replied with a faint, self-satisfied smirk in his voice.

'It's still too early for you to be listed in the book, you see. You've only been living there for a few weeks, after all. But the operator was most helpful.'

She tried attack as her best form of defence. 'I suppose you think you've been very clever.'

'No, not really. I've been a bit too concerned for that.'

'Concerned? That my cheque might bounce, you mean?' She regretted saying it the moment the words had left her lips. She was being grossly unfair now, and she knew it. 'I . . . I'm sorry, I didn't mean — '

'Dani, what *is* this all about? And just what is this blasted cheque for?'

'You mean you really don't know?'

'If I knew, I wouldn't need to ask. *Or* send you flowers as a peace-offering.'

She began to wish for a hole that might open up and swallow her. 'I think perhaps you'd better come round,' she said in a low, embarrassed tone. 'I never was much good at apologizing over the phone.'

It was all a mistake, of course. Ben *had* sent her the pictures as a memento of that warm June evening in Nottinghamshire. But the lady he employed part-time to deal with his accounts, having seen the job written down in his work diary, had taken it upon herself to issue an invoice.

Dani crimsoned as his eyes met hers half an hour later. 'Oh, I . . . I'm so sorry, Ben. You must think I'm a complete madwoman.'

He smiled. 'Not a *complete* madwoman,' he said, tearing both the invoice and her cheque up. 'But suppose we forget all this nonsense and start afresh?'

She was surprised that he should want to, considering the way she'd treated him. 'I'd like that,' she said, suddenly feeling better than she had all day. 'And I still owe you a meal.' She paused. 'Do you think they'd allow us back into that Cantonese restaurant?'

'Probably,' he replied with a chuckle. 'But if it's all the same to you, I'd be just as happy with a take-away.'

'Are you sure?'

'Of course. It's always been my experience that the food's not half as important as the person you share it with.'

* * *

From that moment on their relationship blossomed. Gradually each grew relaxed and comfortable in the other's company. They discovered much in common, and in the weeks that followed spent even more time together. They attended photography exhibitions, fashion shows, the odd party, or drove out into the country. They found wild new places and Ben worked his way through one roll of film after another, capturing them all for posterity.

Under his guidance, Dani's previously-limited confidence flourished. Whenever one or the other of them was out of town on an assignment, they kept in touch by phone. For Dani it was a wonderful, wonderful time, full of fun and contentment and deep-red roses, which Ben bestowed upon her regularly, and with an impetuosity she hadn't dreamed he could possess.

There was never any conscious decision between them to fall in love. Like their relationship itself, the emotion just developed naturally. Neither of them even thought to discuss the wonderful magic between them until one rainy evening in October.

It had been a rest-day for both of them, and Ben had asked her if she would like to meet his father, Brian. Brian, now a widower, lived in a beautiful Chiltern cottage in the equally picturesque village of Newminster, about ten miles outside Maidstone, in Kent. At first Dani had been apprehensive, because, like any proud parent, she felt sure Ben's father would want only the best for his son, and be especially critical of the girl he was dating.

But such did not prove to be the case. Brian Tremain turned out to be a sweet-natured sixty-year-old full of old-world charm who made her feel welcome as soon as Ben introduced them. Together they spent a pleasant afternoon in Brian's cosy little sitting-room, drinking tea and chatting like old friends, until at length Ben glanced at his watch and said they'd better be going.

That evening they went to see a film, and from there Ben drove Dani back through the rainy streets in silence. She knew something was on his mind, and knew also that he would tell her what it was when he felt the time was right.

That time came when he saw her to her front door.

It was quite late; after eleven. Around them, the sleeping house was silent. Only the distant sounds of the rain and the occasional passing car broke the hush.

Ben looked down into her eyes and

more or less *communicated* his feelings to her. Then, to make sure there was no misunderstanding between them, he reached out and placed his hands on her arms.

'Every man's entitled to make a fool of himself once in his lifetime,' he said quietly. 'I think tonight that time has come for me.'

Dani gazed up into his face. Her pulse was racing and her mouth was dry. She, too, had sensed something different in their relationship today, as if they were about to cross that invisible line that stops friends from being lovers.

He cleared his throat. He wore that grim, vaguely troubled look he usually reserved for work, but tonight it was softened by a hint of uncertainty. 'You've become very important to me in the last couple of months,' he said. 'I know it sounds ridiculous, but I've grown to live only for the times when we're together.' A quirky smile touched his lips. 'There — that *does* sound foolish, doesn't it?'

She shook her head. 'No. Not at all.'

'Well, if that doesn't,' he said, 'how about this? I love you, Dani. And I want to spend the rest of my life with you — if you'll have me.'

Even though she'd guessed some of what he was going to say, his softly-spoken words still brought tears flooding to her eyes. 'Oh, Ben . . . ' Emotion stopped her from saying more, and she reached up to hug him, feeling safe in his firm embrace.

At last she recovered her senses sufficiently to speak. 'Oh, Ben. I love you too. For weeks, now.'

Their kiss, when it came, was a soft meeting of lips, gentle but urgent, and electric with restrained passion. Dani felt warmth radiating from Ben's skin, felt his light stubble rubbing pleasurably against her cheek, smelled his fresh, natural scent and basked unashamedly in his love.

He held her tighter, until she pushed herself back a little so that she could look up into his handsome face. '*I* want nothing more than to spend *my* life with *you*, Ben. I want to be yours.' Much to his surprise, she gave a tearful chuckle. 'I *am* yours,' she whispered. 'Yours for eternity.'

'Dani . . .'

They kissed again.

Eternity. It had sounded like such a long time, then. But it wasn't. It was pitifully, painfully short. Because, that very same night —

★   ★   ★

Abruptly Dani closed the book on her past. She had reminisced enough for one day, and while the memories of those first few months with Ben still filled her with a joy it was difficult to contain, the recollection of what came afterwards broke her heart.

Dani consulted her watch. Somehow the afternoon had flown past, and the working day was almost over.

Her sigh filled the small office.

Although she had assured Colin earlier that she was fine, she had to confess that maybe she *was* feeling a little under the weather.

Wearily she packed a few papers and documents into her briefcase. Enough was enough. She would go home and finish off these few odds and ends in the comfort of her flat.

The watery late-April afternoon was gloomy and overcast as she stepped out of the building and into the car-park. A chilly breeze had blown up, too. She went over to her car, unlocked it, put her briefcase on the back seat and then climbed in herself. Within moments she was steering the car out into the busy road.

Although she didn't want to think about her time with Ben any longer, the memories still crowded into her head. She tried to blot them out by concentrating on her driving, but now that the floodgates of her mind had been opened, they were proving difficult to close again.

That night, after they had confessed their love for each other, and spent a very happy hour discussing some of the ways they would spend the rest of their lives together, Ben had left for his own flat, on the other side of the capital.

There in the hallway, watching him shrug into his jacket, Dani had debated whether or not she should ask him to stay the night. They would never find a more romantic moment, with rain beating a steady tattoo at the window and a distant church clock tolling midnight.

But something stopped her. Maybe she was being prudish and old-fashioned, but whatever happened between them would only *really* feel right once they had made a commit-ment to each other in the eyes of God.

Ben glanced down at her and smiled. At once she coloured. He seemed to have the uncanny knack of reading her thoughts. Taking her gently into his arms, he kissed her lightly on the forehead. 'I'm not at all tired,' he said.

'And I'm in no mood to get in my car and drive all the way home. But if I don't go *now*, I'll never go. And that would spoil everything, wouldn't it?'

She paused, then nodded. 'I think so.'

At the front door they kissed again, and hugged each other affectionately. 'I'll give you a call tomorrow,' he promised.

When he was gone, Dani went into her living-room and sat before the fire. There were no words apt enough to describe her happiness. She wanted to phone home and share her joy with her parents, but reminded herself that it was now well after midnight.

Reluctantly she decided that she, too, should be in bed. Although she felt too excited to sleep, she had a photo session tomorrow afternoon at which she would be modelling a cardigan for a knitting-pattern. It would do her career no good at all to turn up sleepy-eyed and lethargic.

The following morning, as she prepared for work, Dani willed the phone to ring. It seemed so long since she had last heard Ben's voice. But the phone remained stubbornly silent.

Although she was disappointed, she reminded herself that Ben had a career, too. She couldn't expect him to drop everything just to call her. He led such a hectic life that he would probably have to choose his moment.

Most of her day was spent at a studio in north London, baking beneath strong lights in order to model the smart navy-blue cardigan. On the surface the job looked so easy, but it proved to be demanding, and by the time Dani returned to her flat she was worn out.

She took a bath, hoping that Ben wouldn't ring while she was soaking. As soon as she was dried and dressed again, she began once more to anticipate his call. But still the phone remained silent.

At seven o'clock she began to wonder what could possibly be keeping him so busy. Going over to the phone, she lifted the receiver and checked for a dialling tone. It came through loud and clear. Her phone wasn't out of order, then.

By eight-thirty pique was beginning to mix with worry. Anything could have kept Ben from ringing, of course, even the most innocent of events. But he had become so precious to her . . .

At last she rang his flat. The phone at the other end of the line rang and rang, but nobody came to answer it.

Perhaps Ben was working late. Perhaps he was on his way over to *see* her! She put the handset down and went into the living-room, anticipating the possibility of his visit.

The phone began to ring.

At last!

Dani rushed to answer it. 'Hello, Ben? I've — '

'Danielle?'

For just a second the unfamiliar male voice flustered her. 'Uh, yes, speaking — '

'It's Ben's father here. Brian.'

Dani frowned. How had he got her number? And why was he calling? 'Oh, hello, Mr Tremain. There's . . . ' Her mouth suddenly dried up. 'There's nothing *wrong*, is there?'

Brian's pause was lengthy. 'I'm afraid there's been an accident,' he said after a moment. 'Last night.' Another pause. 'I'm sorry it's taken me so long to contact you, but I've been here at the hospital practically all day.'

Dani's vision swam in and out of focus. She closed her eyes. 'What — ?'

'It was a car crash,' Brian said in a worn-out voice. 'Some drunk-driver jumping a red light.' She heard his sharp, painful intake of breath clearly.

'Is Ben . . . I mean, will he — '

'He's holding on,' Brian replied. 'Just. But I . . . I think it's only fair to tell you exactly what the doctors have told *me*, Danielle. It doesn't look good, my dear. Ben has broken practically every bone in his body and he's gone into . . . into coma. It's just a question of time, the doctors say. Just a question of time until . . . '

He could restrain his sob no longer.

Dani opened her eyes. Immediately big silver tears began streaming down her suddenly-bloodless cheeks. 'What . . . what hospital are you at? I'll be there as soon as I can.'

5

The hospital smelled of soap and antiseptic. The brightly-lit corridors held about them an air of organized chaos. With her hands a-tremble, Dani phoned for a mini-cab and arrived twenty minutes later, to be greeted on the steps of the huge Victorian building by Ben's father.

Brian shared his son's long, lean build. In his pale-grey trousers and dark-blue blazer, he looked tall, slim and worn out. His eyes — a deeper blue than Ben's — appeared lustreless and bloodshot. His long, hollow face was pale and lined.

They shared a brief, encouraging hug. Then Brian said, 'Come on, I'll take you upstairs.'

As he led her past the reception and over to a big, stainless-steel elevator, he said, 'It was good of you to come, Danielle.'

'I had to.'

He nodded. 'I had another word with the doctor just after I rang off from you. It seems that Ben's condition has stabilized. But don't build your hopes up. That only means he isn't getting any *worse*. He's still in a bad way.'

Dani's stomach clenched. She had no idea what to expect as they stepped out of the lift on the sixth floor and Brian led her along a pale-green corridor and through a set of double doors. Her thoughts were only on Ben now, and how cruel fate must be to snatch him away from the promise of so much happiness.

Brian paused to hold a whispered conversation with a nurse sitting at a desk. The nurse said something and nodded. Then Brian took Dani by the arm and led her further along the corridor until they came to a room marked with the number 602. 'I'd prepare myself, if I were you,' he said gravely.

He opened the door and they went inside.

The room was crammed with all kinds of hi-tech machinery. The figure in the single bed — it seemed so difficult to think of it as Ben — was hooked up to it by a jumble of tubes and wiring. Dani went forward to stand at the foot of the bed. She peered down at the still body beneath the sheets.

Ben was swathed in bandages. Only his face was visible. His skin was paper-white, and marked here and there by tiny scratches. His chest rose and fell slowly, reflecting the depth of slumber into which he had fallen.

In her mind's eye, Dani saw him laughing, smiling, looking right into her very soul with his marvellous intensity. Then the citrus scent of his aftershave was replaced by the sharp smell of antiseptic and her vision suddenly dissolved as tears filled her eyes. 'Oh, Ben . . .'

Brian came forward and put his hands on her shoulders, and she turned, sobbing, to bury her face in his chest.

★ ★ ★

That evening became a timeless blur. After a while Brian took her to a waiting-room at the far end of the corridor and bought them both coffee from a vending machine. They sat in silence for a time, then went back to look in on Ben.

There had been no change.

'Look, you'd better get along home,' Brian said kindly as they stood at the foot of the bed. 'Ben's condition has stabilized, so presumably, the worst is over. There's not much either of us can do now, except pray — and we can do that anywhere.'

Dani looked up at the older man. 'What . . . what about you?'

He sighed. 'I'll hang on for a while.'

'I'll keep you company.'

'No. Really. You've got a career to think about, commitments. I'm retired, don't forget. My time's my own.'

She swallowed and nodded. Although it was difficult to keep track of such things at a time like this, she knew that tomorrow was going to be a busy day for her, finishing off the knitting-pattern job in the morning and auditioning for a poster campaign to advertise word processors in the afternoon. 'All right. If you're sure.'

'I am.'

It was well past midnight when she rang for a mini-cab and returned to her flat. Despite her exhaustion, however, she was too upset to sleep very well. She rose early the following morning, telephoned the number Brian had given her before they parted, and asked the nurse at the other end of the line about Ben's condition. The nurse told her that there was no change.

Without much enthusiasm, Dani set about preparing herself for the day's work. Her reflection looked pale and preoccupied as she applied blusher and lipstick. Her thoughts were only of Ben, and what should happen if —

When the doorbell rang, she jumped. Glancing at her watch, she saw that the time was almost seven-thirty. Going out into the hallway, she opened the door to reveal a smiling young man all but lost in a thick, fur-lined parka.

'Miss McMasters, is it?' he asked.

Surprised, for the caller was a complete stranger to her, Dani nodded. 'Can I help you?' she asked warily.

He said yes, she could. 'You knew Ben Tremain, I understand.'

At once she stiffened, fearing the worst. 'I *know* Ben, yes.'

'According to my sources, you were lovers,' he said.

Now Dani was *really* taken aback. 'I — Who *are* you?'

'Dave Simpson,' the fair-haired young man replied, still smiling. He produced a card from one of his many pockets identifying him as a staff writer for a trade newspaper specializing in fashion and photography. 'I wonder if I could ask you a few questions? Tremain was one of the photography world's most promising young talents, and I've been asked to report his acci — '

Dani shook her head. 'No, I — '

'I understand that you and Mr Tremain were lovers,' he interrupted, repeating the allegation again.

Taken by surprise, Dani felt confused and uncertain how best to deal with this persistent reporter. 'We *know* each other, yes.'

'And he met with his accident after leaving your flat in the wee small hours, am I right?'

She bristled. 'What is that supposed to mean?'

That infuriating smile of his grew wider. 'I'm only trying to fill in some background.'

'It sounds to me as if you're trying to turn what happened into something scandalous.'

Simpson shrugged. 'Look, I've been assigned to write three hundred words for Friday's edition, and I'm looking for an angle. My sources tell me you and

Tremain have been keeping company for the past few months, so I've come here to get a few quotes.'

On the surface he sounded quite plausible, she thought. But Dani did not trust the look in his hooded eyes. 'I'm sorry, but I have no comments to make — '

'I just wondered,' Simpson said artfully, before she could close the door on him. 'Tremain's always been something of a loner. Suddenly he finds himself a girlfriend and *wham*! He has a car crash. Makes you wonder, doesn't it? About his concentration, I mean. Whether or not he had . . . *other* things on his mind.'

Dani's face tingled as colour came into her cheeks. 'If you're trying to imply that *I* was the cause of the accident — '

'*Were* you? Did you have an argument or something? Had you just split up?'

'A drunken driver caused that crash!'

'Yeah, sure, I know. But like I say, I'm

109

looking for an angle — '

'Well, you won't find it here!' she snapped, feeling her lower lip tremble as tears came to her eyes. 'Now get away from my doorstep or I'll call the police!'

She slammed the door with a sound like thunder.

* * *

No change.

Over the next three weeks Dani grew to hate those words, because what they really meant, of course, was *no improvement.*

The majority of Ben's bones slowly mended and the tiny glass-cuts on his pale face gradually healed, but Ben himself remained in coma, insensible, unmoved by events around him.

Dani spent as much time at his bedside as she could, just talking softly to him and studying his ghostly profile. Whenever she was called away by other commitments, Brian took over. Both of them began to resemble the man in the bed. They lost their appetites, and consequently lost weight. Dark rings developed beneath their dull eyes. Worry turned them into pale images of their former selves.

Meanwhile, despite the best efforts of the hospital staff, Ben continued to lie in coma.

Somehow the days passed, but Brian knew that things couldn't go on this way. A month had elapsed since the accident, but judging by the way it had aged Dani, it might as well have been a decade. The poor girl was virtually a somnambulist herself, just going through the motions, neglecting everything around her and living — if such a twilight existence could be *called* living — only for the hours she could spend sitting at Ben's side, and talking of things in their past that might suddenly reawaken his sleeping mind.

Six weeks after the accident, with the world beyond the door of room 602 preparing for Christmas, Brian finally decided that enough was enough. 'Dani, you can't go on like this. You're running yourself into the ground.'

She looked up at him through slightly-glazed eyes, almost as if she were having difficulty in understanding him. 'Does that matter?' she asked tiredly. 'I've got to be there for him, Brian. When he wakes up, I've got to be there.'

Although the words nearly choked him, Brian had to say them. '*If* he wakes up, you mean.'

'*Brian* — !'

'There are no guarantees, Dani. Oh, of course I still have hope. Without that I've got nothing. But let's be realistic for a moment. The chances of us ever getting Ben back — the Ben we both knew and loved, I mean — grow slimmer with every day that passes.'

They were talking in the sixth floor waiting-room. It was late at night and they had it to themselves. Now, the harsh fluorescent lights overhead illuminated Dani's look of outrage. 'How can you *say* such a thing, Brian? How can you even *think* it? Of course Ben will come back to us. He *has* to!'

He shook his head and ran one hand through his short, black-grey hair, then reached out and hugged her paternally. 'You're a marvellous young lady. Ben loves you dearly, and I can see why. But if you make *yourself* ill, what good will you be to Ben if . . . *when* . . . he recovers consciousness?' He held her at arm's length. 'You can't spend your every day here. We could wait a year before he shows even the faintest signs of recovery, maybe longer . . . ' He swallowed hard. 'You've got to go back out into the world, pick up your career and get on with your life.' His eyes held hers. '*That* is what Ben would want you to do; go back out into the world and make him proud of you.'

Dani looked down at the plain blue tiles beneath their feet. She felt exhausted and confused, but had to concede that Brian was probably right. She knew that Ben would want her to justify his faith in her as a model.

Suddenly she realized that she must look a mess, that she probably had done ever since the evening she'd first received the bad news . . .

She looked up into Brian's parchment-like face. It was going to be hard, returning to the life she'd all but forsaken six weeks before. She had adapted to this near-constant bedside vigil, and on a purely emotional level was loath to leave it. But Brian was right; Ben would want her to be strong, and she would be — for *him*.

* * *

Gradually she eased herself back into her modelling career. The dark rings beneath her eyes faded and a hint of colour came back into her cheeks. She took as many of the most demanding assignments as she could, because for her work was now medicine.

She spent time at the hospital as often as she was able — she and Brian even spent Christmas Day at Ben's bedside — and slowly her mind readjusted itself once again to finally accept what had happened, and, however difficult, to make the best of it.

In early January she received a call from the modelling agency. Judging by her tone, Cheryl was obviously excited about something.

Beau Monde, the company for whom Dani had done the Nottinghamshire shoot six months before, were preparing a new, more lavish catalogue — to be photographed throughout Europe. It was, Cheryl stressed, a job she would be foolish to turn down.

'Well . . . yes,' Dani agreed. 'I suppose it is. But . . . Europe. I mean, it seems so far away, and I don't want to travel too far because of Ben . . .'

'I understand that,' Cheryl replied. 'But it would be good for you, Dani. And it might interest you to know that Colin Howard himself specifically asked that you be involved. I think you must have impressed him more than he let on during that last shoot.'

Dani considered. It certainly was a golden opportunity. But she didn't really believe she could bring herself to accept it with any degree of professionalism. 'I'd be forever worrying, Cheryl . . . It would probably be more trouble than it's worth . . . '

'Well, why don't you think about it tonight, and give me a definite answer tomorrow?'

'All right, I will. Thanks.'

'Go,' Brian said without hesitation later that afternoon. 'This girl at the agency's right, it will do you the world of good, and heaven knows, you could use a change of scene. It would get those so-called reporters off your back, too.'

That was certainly true. Dave Simpson had continued to pester her off and on, as had two or three local newspapers circulated in the area where Ben had lived.

'But a *month*, Brian. That's how long I'll be gone. And if anything should happen, I couldn't just fly back home. I'd be committed — '

'Nothing will happen that we don't *pray* will happen — I hope,' he said with a brave attempt at optimism. 'And in any case, I know you'll be with us in spirit.'

Dani was still undecided. According to the doctors, there were some complications with the injuries to Ben's back and neck —

'Go,' Brian urged again. 'Ben would want you to, you know that. And a prestige job like this could open up all kinds of new opportunities for you.'

When her parents offered similar, sound advice, Dani knew she would be a fool to ignore it. The following morning, she phoned the agency and asked Cheryl how soon Beau Monde wanted her to be ready to fly out.

* * *

The four weeks she spent in Europe were, as everyone had predicted,

117

marvellous. Once more, Dani was part of a small group of models. Their schedule was hectic, their work demanding. But the constantly-changing vistas, languages and customs, plus the valued companionship of the other girls, proved to be just the tonic she needed.

Invariably, of course, her thoughts returned to Ben. That she was so many miles from home when Ben was so ill often made her feel guilty, but somehow Colin Howard was always on hand to cheer her up.

In any case, there was fortunately little time for introspection. Their whistle-stop tour began in France, then slowly moved up through Belgium, the Netherlands and West Germany. The photographer Colin had hired for the shoot was older than Ben, but no less professional. He, too, was gifted with the power to conjure up the exact mood or expression he desired, and everyone got along well with him.

The shoot finished three days ahead of schedule, by which time everyone was anxious to return home. Dani had sent postcards and letters whenever possible, but they were a poor substitute for actual contact with her loved ones, and as she packed for the flight home, she felt her spirits lift in anticipation of a wonderful reunion.

The previous afternoon, she had sent a wire to the small London hotel at which Brian had decided to stay while Ben was in hospital, just to let him know of their revised travel plans. Early the following morning, the entire Beau Monde entourage travelled by train to Findel Airport, some six kilometres east of Luxembourg, and caught British Airways' eight o'clock flight to London.

Heathrow Airport was bustling when the plane touched down a couple of hours later. As Colin hurried them all through Customs, Dani saw so many different nationalities represented by the people crowding around her that it was almost as if she were visiting a world within a world.

When they finally reached a reasonably peaceful section of Terminal One, Colin told them to wait while he tried to locate their baggage. As the minutes passed, a few of the other girls were greeted by boyfriends or parents. Dani watched all the hugs and smiles with a mixture of pleasure and envy.

It suddenly occurred to her to find a phone booth and ring the hospital to check on Ben's condition.

Before she could put the thought into action, however, she heard a male voice call her name. For one heart-stopping moment she thought it belonged to Ben, that Ben had recovered and come to meet her himself. Then she spun around and saw Brian standing thirty feet away, waving to attract her attention.

His expression telegraphed the bad news ahead.

As she hurried through the crowd to reach him, all the babble around them seemed to fade away. No longer was she aware of the other travellers, the chaos, the constant buzz of chatter or the deafening roar of planes flying low overhead.

'Ben — ' she began as soon as she reached the older man.

Brian swallowed. 'I'm sorry, Dani,' he said, stepping forward to take her into his protective embrace. 'Ben . . . Ben died a fortnight ago.'

All the colour was sponged from her face as she shook her head. 'No . . . no . . . '

'It's true, my dear,' he said quietly, his own dark blue eyes moist and troubled. 'I . . . I decided not to contact you when it happened because I knew Ben wouldn't have wanted you to miss out on such a wonderful opportunity, and neither did I.'

Ben dead? Dani's mind refused to accept the fact. 'What? Why — ?'

'The doctors did all they could,' Brian told her, looking straight into her face now, so that she *had* to accept what he was saying. 'But there were complications, his spine and neck . . . '

A tortured moan escaped from her. 'Oh, no! God, no . . . *please!*'

'We held the funeral last week,' Brian said, hugging her paternally as she began to cry. 'I'm sorry, Dani. Truly sorry.'

She heard nothing more as grief claimed her entirely. The only sound was the awful, empty silence of her heart, breaking.

⋆ ⋆ ⋆

There, Dani thought, now firmly back in the present. Despite her best efforts to stifle those still-vivid memories, they had played themselves through her mind yet again. And, just like always, they had served no purpose other than to torment her.

As she pulled into the gravel drive leading up to the smart apartment block in which she now lived, she wondered how many times during the past six years she had believed her aching heart to have finally mended.

Too many, she decided almost at once. And every time she had been wrong. There was always something, or someone, to reawaken that time in her life when her sweet dream had turned into a nightmare.

She switched off the engine of her ice-green Metro and released her seat-belt. She'd often thought that perhaps she had finally come to terms with losing Ben. After the initial shock and a grey and desperate period of mourning, she had gone back to work, or rather, *tried* to. But she only had to see a camera to find herself remembering the tall, raven-haired man to whom she had promised herself for eternity, so work became impossible.

Colin Howard had come to her rescue again, she recalled as she climbed out of her car and reached for her briefcase. He had offered her a job at Beau Monde, which, by then, was beginning to expand at a surprising rate.

She had accepted gratefully, because

it meant that she could still work with fashion without having to face the cameras and lights that so reminded her of the tragedy which had all but shattered her young life.

She had worked hard and diligently, and been rewarded for her commitment to BM. Her position now, as chief fashion buyer, gave her enormous satisfaction . . . until times such as this came upon her. Then she would find herself thinking constantly of Ben, and what they might have shared, and a feeling of restlessness would come over her so strong that sometimes she felt it would drive her mad.

As she walked from the car to the front door of the modern, tan-brick building, the clouds which had been gathering steadily during the course of her drive back from town began to release a light drizzle. Although it was only four-thirty, it was already quite dark. She pressed the security number on the front door to let herself inside, then crossed the tiled reception and took her key from her handbag.

As she opened her door she thought she heard a strange, muffled sound from within. Immediately she was on her guard, for she was expecting no visitors — especially none who could let themselves into her flat in her absence.

Without stepping across the threshold, she called out, 'Who's there? Who is it?'

Again she heard a sound inside the darkened flat — footsteps hurrying across the living-room floor!

'Who's there?' she called again, certain now that her unknown intruder had been up to no good.

Then her keen hearing picked out a new sound. It took her a moment to identify it. All at once she realized that whoever was in her flat — almost without doubt a burglar — was making his escape through the French windows in the dining-room.

The knowledge that she had scared the thief into a hurried retreat bolstered her courage, but just wondering what damage he had already wrought, and what he might already have stolen, still left her breathless and trembling.

Reaching just inside the front door, she snapped on the hallway light. 'I'm warning you . . . ' she began.

But there was no sound at all now, save that of ticking clocks and the drizzle outside, and instinctively she knew that her uninvited guest was gone.

Now that it was all over, she felt quite dizzy. She leaned against the doorframe for a moment, getting her breath back. When she heard a man's voice behind her she cried out and twisted around.

'Are you all right, Dani? I heard you calling out . . . '

Her shoulders fell in a sigh of relief. It was Mr Berner, a retired civil servant who lived next door. His lined face was serious with concern, and he held a stick of wood at the ready in his right hand.

'I think I've just been burgled,' she replied.

His scowl deepened. He and his wife

had grown very protective of her during the three years they'd been neighbours. 'You do, do you?' he asked. 'Well, we'll soon see about that.'

'Be careful,' she warned.

Together they entered the flat, switching on lights as they went. Dani saw that a few odds and ends had been shifted around, but nothing appeared to be missing.

Sure enough, they found the French windows open. This was obviously the way the burglar had gained entry, too. They saw that he had used a glass-cutter to remove three small sections of glass from the right-hand door, at the top, middle and bottom, then reached inside to release the bolts and turn the key in the lock.

'I'll call the police,' Mr Berner announced when they had finished checking all the rooms.

'Thank you,' Dani replied distantly. 'Although I'm not sure that they'll take the matter any further. Nothing seems to be missing. A few of my personal papers have been disturbed, but that's about all.'

'True,' Mr Berner agreed. 'Still, they'd better be told.'

Dani nodded, already back in deep thought, pondering the identity of the burglar — and what he had been hoping to find.

6

At the other end of the line, Kate Allison's voice was full of concern. 'Oh, Dani, how terrible!'

It was the following morning, and Dani had phoned the office to let her assistant know that she would be working from home today, while she waited for a locksmith and glazier to come out and make the necessary changes and repairs to her doors and windows.

'Well, it could have been worse,' Dani replied philosophically. 'I mean, nothing was stolen, and apart from these three draughty holes in my French windows, the place wasn't vandalized at all.'

'Still, it must have been an awful shock,' said Kate.

'I was shook up at the time, I don't mind telling you. But fortunately I have two very protective neighbours, and they kept me company for most of the evening, and calmed me down with endless cups of tea.'

'What did the police have to say about it?'

'Not a great deal. They told me that they suspected that whoever he was, the burglar was a professional. He let himself in without alerting anyone else, and he didn't leave any fingerprints behind him.'

'But you say he didn't take anything, either.'

'The police think I disturbed him before he had a chance to make off with anything of value,' Dani explained. For some reason even she could not understand, she chose not to tell Kate what else the police had said; that perhaps the thief had been looking for something in particular that he either couldn't locate, or wasn't there in the first place. 'Anyway, it's all over and done with now — or it will be as soon as the locksmith and glazier arrive.'

'Well, I'll certainly pass the news on to Colin, but don't be in any rush to come back to work,' Kate said, still obviously concerned. 'You could use a break. What with that business at the reception the other day, this hasn't been your week.'

'We'll see, Kate. Call me if you run into any problems.'

'I will. Bye.'

Dani put the phone down and gazed thoughtfully at the three neat squares which had been cut from the right-hand door of her French windows. Who *was* the intruder? What *had* he been after? And was he by any chance connected to the driver of the mysterious white car that had followed her the previous morning?

She recalled some of the last words Kate had spoken, about 'that business at the reception the other day . . . ' What she'd meant, of course, was Dani's claim to have seen a man who had died six years earlier.

She closed her hazel eyes. She knew

she should just let the matter drop. It had been a simple case of mistaken identity, as she herself had told Colin. But what if it *wasn't*?

She cast her mind back to the reception. Again she saw the man who had given her such a shock. She saw his lively blue eyes, his firm, straight mouth, his square jaw pitted by an appealing dimple —

It *was* Ben, she felt certain. But how *could* it be? Everyone had a double, so they said. But was such an uncanny resemblance possible between two people presumably unrelated by blood?

She stood up and moved about the room in frustration. This line of thought was getting her nowhere. Ben was dead, it was as simple as that.

The doorbell rang and Dani padded outside to answer it. A florid-faced man in blue overalls announced himself as the locksmith.

Dani stood aside. 'Oh, come in. Can I get you a cup of tea?'

The locksmith nodded gratefully. 'If

it's no trouble.' He glanced around the flat with professional interest. 'It's all the locks you want changing, is it?'

'Yes — and locks fitted to all the windows as well, if that's possible.'

'Oh, I think we can manage that,' the man said good-naturedly.

While Dani went into the kitchen, the locksmith set to work. Twenty minutes later the glazier arrived, measured up the three panes of glass he would need to replace, then drove off to get them cut.

Sitting at the kitchen table, Dani opened her briefcase. For obvious reasons, she hadn't even touched the work she had brought home with her the previous evening. Now she resolved to put her time at home to good use and deal with it.

She arranged all her paperwork in a neat stack and began to work her way through. Here was an invoice for fabric that she would have to query with BM's accountant, there a reminder to contact a manufacturer whose normally high standards of dressmaking had started to slip just recently.

Dani worked slowly through the pile, looking up once, when the glazier returned and went to work in the dining-room.

About three-quarters of an hour later, she came to a lengthy list of names and addresses and frowned. It was the guest-list Colin had prepared for the reception they'd held in central London the day before yesterday.

There was no reason she could think of for having put it into her briefcase. More than likely she had picked it up with some other papers by mistake.

She was just about to put it aside when she remembered part of the conversation she'd had with Colin just after she'd regained consciousness in the rest-room of the Playfair Hotel. She had told him that she'd seen Ben, and he had replied by saying that if Ben *had* been there, then he, Colin, would have seen him as well.

'*There were three hundred people at*

the reception, Colin,' she'd argued. 'You couldn't have noticed all of them.'

And he had replied, 'True. But not one of those three hundred people could have got in without an invite, Dani, and who would have thought to send an invite out to . . .'

Colin's voice had trailed off then, but now Dani finished the question for him. Who would have thought to send an invite out to a dead man?

Suddenly she was fired by a determination to find out. To settle this business once and for all.

Taking a fluorescent pink marker-pen, she began to work her way through the list. The majority of the guests had been women, and these she discounted immediately. Then she worked her way through all the men, highlighting their names if she knew, or knew of, them.

Half an hour later she sat back and rubbed at her eyes. She had accounted for all but seven of the male guests. But at no time had Ben's name cropped up on the list.

Undaunted, she resolved to find out exactly who these seven unknown male guests really were. But how was she going to do that? Ring them? That was one option. But what would she say when she finally got through to them?

It was then that she settled upon a new course of action. She could save herself a great deal of work and unnecessary embarrassment by going directly to the one person who could give her the truth — Ben's father, Brian.

She and Brian had kept in touch for a while, after that dreadful meeting at Heathrow Airport, but with Brian now back in his beautiful little village in Kent, and Dani slowly picking up the pieces of her life, their only contact had soon trickled down to the odd phone call and Christmas card. She realized now that they hadn't actually spoken for more than three years.

But if anyone should know the truth of the matter, it was Brian. And with her heart pounding madly, Dani went in search of her address-book, to find his number and give him a call.

'Hmmm!' she muttered fifteen minutes later.

'Problem, lady?' asked the glazier, busy fitting his third pane of glass.

Dani glanced around and forced herself to smile. 'Oh, no, it's nothing. I seem to have mislaid my address-book, that's all.'

Well, that put paid to her plans to call Brian, she thought. Unless, of course, he was listed in the telephone directory. For a moment she couldn't decide whether she felt relieved or disappointed. But then it occurred to her that perhaps a personal visit would be better than a rather *im*personal telephone call. For one thing, she would actually be able to *watch* Brian's reactions to her questions. Over the phone she would have to set too much store by the tone of his voice alone.

A personal visit, then, she decided with a peculiar mixture of excitement and apprehension. This very afternoon, after the workmen had gone.

*　*　*

The thought of actually doing something positive to end her uncertainty once and for all left Dani feeling anxious and impatient. Part of her knew that Ben *was* dead, that this idea in her mind that he might somehow still be alive was just wishful thinking. But then again, she had to believe the evidence of her own eyes, too — and she knew exactly what she had seen at the reception two days before.

After the locksmith and glazier departed, she glanced up at the living-room clock. It was lunchtime, but she felt too nervous to even contemplate food. Again she considered her plan. It was impulsive, yes. But there was no time for hesitation. Should she think about it too much, she would probably abandon it altogether.

Still, there were so many possibilities

to take into account. What if Brian had moved, or, God forbid, passed away himself? Supposing he *was* still living at the cosy Chiltern cottage she remembered so well. Would her visit and subsequent line of questioning cause him too much distress?

She could not possibly answer her own questions, of course. She would just have to take a chance and deal with events as they happened.

Picking up her car-keys, she checked her appearance briefly in the hallway mirror. She was wearing a pale-pink cardigan over a white blouse and smart stone-washed jeans. For a moment she considered changing into more formal attire, then decided against it. It would take too long, for one thing, and she had quite a drive ahead of her.

Leaving the flat, she hurried over to her car. The weather was brighter today. The misty grey clouds which had made the previous day so gloomy had been chased away by a brisk westerly wind.

Dani got into the car, clipped her

seat-belt shut, started the engine and took a series of deep breaths to steady her racing pulse. For better or worse, she knew she must go through with her plan, or continue to suffer the uncertainty which was blighting her whole life.

With her face a mask of determination, she put the car into first gear and set out on the long drive to Kent.

★ ★ ★

It was an awkward, circuitous journey until she picked up the M25 at Chertsey. After that it was just a case of following the motorway east, until it became the M26.

Now driving required only the minimum of thought and concentration, and she felt doubt insinuating itself into her mind once again. With slightly less resolve than that she had shown back at her flat, she banished the indecision from her thoughts once more, but she knew that if she didn't reach her destination soon, she might very well forsake her plan altogether.

At last she found herself on the M20. Her journey was nearing its completion. She left the motorway at Aylesford, and began to look out for signs that would lead her on to the village of Newminster.

It was only then, glancing up into her rear-view mirror, that she spotted the mysterious white car following her again.

The Metro veered a little across the road as she momentarily lost her concentration. Correcting the steering, she licked her lips. There was no doubt in her mind now. Someone was definitely following her. But who *was* it? And *why* were they doing it?

A sign loomed up on her left. *NEWMINSTER — 2 MILES*. Thank goodness she was almost there! With her heart beating unpleasantly fast, she continued along the quiet country road, hedges and dry-stone walls speeding past in a heady blur of greens and greys.

Now she thought back to her last visit to Brian's home, and began to look out for any familiar landmarks that would guide her to his cottage. A quick glance in the rear-view mirror told her that the white car had once again disappeared from sight.

Ten minutes later she pulled up outside the picturesque cottage she remembered so well. She switched off the engine and sat there for a minute or so, just listening to the tranquillity of the sleeping lane. Climbing out of the car, she cleared her throat. What awaited her behind those neatly-curtained windows, she wondered. The truth, at last?

There was only one way to find out.

She followed the neat, flower-bordered path up to the front door and reached out to push the bell. For one split second she hesitated, no longer sure that she could actually go through with her plan. Then she pressed the button, and somewhere inside the house she heard a musical chime.

Perhaps Brian *had* moved away. Perhaps she *should* have telephoned ahead, just to make sure. But then all her doubts were dismissed as the front door swung open and Ben's father appeared in the frame.

'Yes? Why, Danielle!'

Was that surprise she saw on his face, or panic? Was her imagination getting the better of her, or had he unwittingly given the impression that he'd been *expecting* her?

'Brian,' she said, genuinely pleased to see him again after so long a gap.

They embraced, then Brian stood aside. 'Well, this is a pleasure,' he said. 'Come in, my dear. I'll make us a pot of tea.'

The last few years had hardly left a mark on him. He still stood tall and slim. His hair was still thick, and held more black than grey. He looked quite dapper in his brown cardigan and beige trousers. Dani stepped inside and he closed the door behind her, then ushered her through to the parlour she remembered so fondly.

'Now, make yourself at home,' he said, guiding her to a fireside chair. 'That's it. I'll just go and put the kettle on. Be back in a moment.'

Dani sat down, enjoying the peaceful sense of 'coming home' despite the tautness of her nerves. Before long, Brian had returned with a tray filled with cups, plates and a hastily-arranged display of cakes and scones.

'There,' he said, placing the tray on the small table between them before taking the chair opposite her. 'Well — what have you been doing with yourself since we last spoke?'

Briefly, Dani told him. She had a great deal of affection for this man. The bond between them had been forged during those long, desperate weeks at Ben's bedside. But she was sure that he was on edge, and equally certain that it was her own sudden appearance which had put him there.

'And how have things been going for you?' she asked, taking a sip of tea to moisten her dry lips.

Brian said that he now had a part-time job, of sorts. 'Odd jobs, mostly,' he explained. 'A spot of gardening here, some decorating there. It all helps to supplement my pension, of course, but more than that, it gets me out of the house and keeps me occupied.'

'You must be very lonely with Ben gone,' she said, watching his face closely.

He averted his eyes. 'Oh, I get by.'

Dani had no wish to play games with him, nor attempt to trick him into admitting the truth. So she forced herself to say what was in her mind as directly as she could. 'Ben's still alive, isn't he?'

Brian's dark blue eyes came up to her face. She thought she saw a struggle of sorts playing across his weathered features. At last he said, 'Yes.'

Even though she had known in her heart of hearts that Ben *couldn't* be alive, she had clung to the hope much as a drowning man might grasp at a straw. But now, as he confirmed the truth she had been so afraid to believe, she felt herself go pale.

'Sit back,' he said, seeing her reaction. He leaned forward and took her cup away from her, and she sank deeper into the chair, breathing through her mouth and willing her jangled senses to settle. 'It's a shock, I know. It's best that you just relax for a while and let it sink in.'

But already a thousand questions were crowding into her mind, and she found herself asking him the most important. 'Why . . . why did you tell me he had died?'

Brian sank back into his own chair. He looked wretched. Between them steam rose from their forgotten teacups like a misty grey curtain. 'You know,' he said, 'I've been expecting this visit. It was only a matter of time.'

'Then I really *did* see Ben at the Playfair Hotel on Monday?'

He nodded. 'It wasn't intentional.

Ben was attending the Beau Monde function on an entirely separate matter. He had no way of knowing that you worked for the company, or that you would be there. It was as much a surprise to him as it evidently was to you.'

'You know that I fainted, then?'

'Yes, Ben told me that evening. He was very upset about it. He left the hotel almost straightaway.'

'You haven't answered my question yet,' she persisted. 'Why did you tell me he was dead, Brian?'

He knew he could postpone the truth no longer. It was written all over his face. So he cleared his throat and said, 'First of all, please believe me when I tell you that I never wanted to deceive you, Dani, and that the only reason that Ben and I did, was to spare you even more heartache than you *did* suffer.'

'I don't think I could have suffered any more than I did,' she replied. 'But go on; I'm listening.'

Brian nodded. 'On the evening before

you flew out to France to begin work on that catalogue-shoot in Europe,' he said, 'Ben came out of his coma.'

'Came out — !'

'Yes. I could hardly believe it myself. He just opened his eyes, looked around and called my name as if he might just have dozed off for an hour or so.

'Well, of course, I was overjoyed. I even left the room in search of a phone, intending to call you with the good news. But then I thought, what if he slipped back into coma? What if his return to consciousness was only temporary? I decided that it was probably best not to raise your hopes.

'As the days wore on, however, it soon became obvious to me that he really *was* on the mend. His thought processes were unaffected, thank goodness, and at no time did he suffer any relapse. To all intents and purposes, he was the same Ben Tremain we both secretly believed we would never see again.'

Dani frowned. 'Then what was the problem?'

'You'll remember that, while the rest of his bones mended quite satisfactorily, there were complications with the injuries to his spine and neck.'

'That's right.'

'Well, they were more complicated than the doctors thought.' He paused. 'Complicated enough to paralyse Ben from the neck down.'

Dani put a shaking hand to her mouth. 'No!'

Brian nodded sadly. 'Of course, we were devastated. Ben had always been so active, as you know. To cheat death, and yet come back to us without the use of his body, seemed doubly unfair.

'It was while you were away in Europe that Ben made up his mind about something which had been worrying him ever since he'd come out of coma. He knew you loved him deeply, and had promised yourself to him for eternity, but he had no desire to ruin your life by foisting himself upon you.'

Dani sat up straight. 'He wouldn't have been foisted upon me! I'd have looked after him willingly!'

'That's as maybe,' Brian said calmly. 'But as far as Ben was concerned, it would have been unfair. You had a life of your own, after all, a flourishing career, too. How could he expect you to forsake all that just to care for him?'

Dani's eyes fell away from his face. She felt confused, relieved, angry and bitter. But she could understand the way Ben must have been thinking all those years before. 'So that's why he decided to 'die',' she prompted quietly. 'For my benefit.'

'Yes. He was quite adamant about it, made me swear to go along with his scheme.'

'Well, you played your role very well, Brian,' she said with a venom she couldn't suppress. 'You were so convincing that I believed you completely.'

'The tears you saw in my eyes that

day at the airport were genuine enough, I promise you,' he said emotionally. 'I was crying out of pity for the love the two of you were losing.'

A new thought struck her. 'What happened then? To Ben, I mean. When I saw him on Monday he looked fine.'

'For two months he lay in his hospital bed, grieving. He just couldn't seem to get over losing you, Dani. I don't believe he ever did. Despite the best efforts of the physiotherapists, his limbs remained frozen. Then we heard of a Harley Street man who had done some marvellous things with spinal injuries, and we consulted him. He examined Ben thoroughly, and decided that maybe he could perform an operation that might free some of the trapped nerves along his lower back and afford him some small degree of movement.' His eyes moistened. 'He did, and the operation was a success.

'But that modest amount of independence wasn't nearly enough for Ben. In the months that followed he pushed himself to the limit in his desire to regain the use of his limbs. There were times when he would give up all hope of ever achieving that goal, and other times when even *I* believed that he could do it.

'It took him twelve long months,' Brian said proudly, 'but to the complete amazement of all his doctors, he finally triumphed.' Now emotion made his voice dry up, and he reached forward and brought his cup to his lips. 'It was a hollow victory, however,' he went on after a pause. 'We were, if you like, undone by our own deceit. Because as far as you were concerned, Ben was dead and buried. How could he come back into your life? How could he come back into *anyone's* life without the news of it somehow filtering back to you?

'Eventually he realized that there was nothing for it but to adopt a new name, and start a new life elsewhere. He went to live in America, and did quite well over there, too, though not at photography but in the magazine business. He always missed home, however, and when the company he works for offered him the chance to come back to England and take control of their special projects division, he couldn't resist. That's why he was at the Beau Monde reception — to see if it might be possible to link a new fashion magazine with a highly-regarded chain of shops.'

'Didn't he think he would be recognized?' Dani asked, still stunned by all that she had heard.

Brian shrugged. 'That was always a possibility, of course. But six years is a long time, Dani, and a new name, a new career . . . '

'*I* recognized him,' she said.

Brian's face clouded. 'Yes,' he said, 'you did. And when he came home that evening, he was more distraught than I'd ever seen him before. You must believe me, Danielle — Ben never meant to cause you any lasting harm. His only wish had always been to *spare* you from grief. But that evening he worried himself sick. You had fainted. Were you all right afterwards? How could he be *sure* you were all right?'

Suddenly something fell into place in Dani's mind. 'So *that's* why — ' she began.

The look on Brian's face suddenly made her fall silent. His troubled blue eyes had shifted to the window — through which she now heard a car slow to a halt.

The older man stood up and peered through the curtain. His face seemed to age. Dani heard footsteps coming up the path outside. 'It's Ben,' he said, obviously agitated.

At once she, too, felt a sudden stab of alarm. She stood up. Although part of her longed to see the man who had so affected her life, another part — the weaker part — wanted only to retreat.

After all these years and all this deceit, how could she possibly face the man to whom she had given her heart? How did she feel about him, now that

she knew the truth? That Ben was alive
. . . it was all so fresh in her mind. She
needed time to let it sink in before she
could even *think* about seeing him
again.

'I . . . I have to go,' she said, hurrying
from the room.

'Danielle!'

'I must!'

As she reached the hallway, she heard
a key turn in the front door lock. She
froze. The door swung open.

She came face to face with Ben.

The years seemed to vanish as she
found herself looking up into the face
she had thought never to see again. As
she had noted at the reception, he had
aged a little, and grown even leaner in
the face and body. But there was little
else about him that had changed. His
thick black hair still swept back from
his forehead, his dusty blue eyes, still
intense, but wiser now and more
mature, shared their intensity with
surprise. For just a moment his dusky
tan seemed to desert him and he turned

pale. His mouth dropped open, revealing his even white teeth, and he spoke her name with the same deep, relaxing quality she remembered so vividly in her dreams.

'D . . . Danielle!'

Her mind became a maelstrom of confusion. She didn't know whether to melt into his arms and thank providence for reuniting them, or run, and keep *on* running, in case the years had changed him inside, and she had to face the knowledge that *her* Ben, the Ben she knew in her *heart*, really *had* died six long years before.

He spoke her name again, as if he couldn't believe she were really there, before him. 'Danielle . . . ?'

And then instinct dictated her actions.

She reached up and slapped him across the face, and he stared down into her moistening eyes with shock. 'What — ?'

'That's for breaking my heart all those years ago,' she said in a voice

156

choked with emotion. Then she slapped him again. 'And *that*,' she sobbed, 'is for sending someone to spy on me instead of being man enough to come forward and confess the truth to me yourself!'

She pushed past him then, unable to hold back her confused tears any longer, and hurried down the path to her car, anxious now to get away from this man she had so longed to find.

7

Dani returned to work the following morning, and applied herself to her various duties with a brisk sense of urgency. For only by immersing herself in the day-to-day running of Beau Monde could she find release from the confusion tormenting her heart and mind. Only in work could she forget about Ben.

But even in this busy atmosphere, dictating memos and letters, phoning suppliers to discuss fabrics and finishings and making decisions which *had* to be right, he still dominated her thoughts.

The fact that he was still alive should have filled her with joy — and it *did*, up to a point. But there was a bitter sense of disappointment in her, too, because she knew better than to believe they could just pick up where they'd left off.

Oh, *she* could, she felt sure. But what about Ben? His father had said that he had never come to terms with losing her. Was it possible, then, that he still felt the same way, too? Or was each of them only in love with the other person as they *used* to be?

Six long years had passed. Both of them had matured, grown in vision and experience. Why, they might just as well be strangers now — and it was that realization that tore her apart.

Still . . . She recalled her meeting with Brian yet again. Evidently Ben had been sufficiently worried about her — still *cared* enough about her — to make certain that she had recovered satisfactorily after fainting at Monday's reception. That was doubtless why he'd employed the driver of the mysterious white car which had been following her ever since Tuesday morning; to make certain that she was over the shock.

But even here confusion reigned, because she didn't know whether to be flattered by his concern, or angry at him for presuming to invade her privacy.

She stood up from her desk and turned to look out over the grey city. Would Ben haunt her forever? Instead of resolving the matter, it appeared she had only made her situation more complicated.

'Hey, I don't pay you an exorbitant wage just to stare out of windows, you know,' said a voice behind her.

She turned and forced a smile as Colin came into the room. Dependable old Colin, she thought. Come what may, she could always rely upon him. 'I'm sorry, I was — '

'Hey, I was only *joking.*'

She sat down again, and as he sat across from her in the visitor's chair, his ruddy, pleasant face sobered. 'What's up, Dani?' he asked in a gentle, sympathetic tone. 'You haven't been right since you came in this morning. Are you still upset about the burglary?'

Burglary? Good Lord, she'd almost *forgotten* about that! 'Oh no, Colin. It's

. . . it's just me, I suppose.'

'Well, you can always confide in me if there's anything troubling you,' he said.

'Yes, I know. And I really appreciate it. It's just . . . ' But how could she tell him about Ben? 'It's just me feeling a little under the weather, I expect,' she finished rather lamely. 'Anyway, what can I do for *you*?'

'This,' he said, putting a letter on the desk. 'I've been meaning to talk to you about it for some time. It's from a fellow called Matthew Daley, who runs the special projects division of Independent International Magazines. Evidently he's planning to launch a new fashion magazine, and he wondered if there was any chance of linking it with us as a way of giving it some credibility in the market-place.'

Dani stared down at the letter, paying special attention to the signature. Yes, she thought, that was Ben's handwriting, all right, and 'Matthew Daley' was the name he'd adopted before going to live in America.

'It sounds like a good idea to me,' Colin went on, apparently oblivious to the subtle shift in Dani's manner. 'But obviously there's a lot to consider before we meet him to discuss it.'

'Meet him?'

Now he did look at her curiously. 'Why, of course. We'd have to meet him if we decided to take him up on his proposition. We'd have to discuss the fee we'd want for the use of our company name, and sign the subsequent agreements. Maybe even push for a say in the magazine's contents — '

'I don't think it's a good idea,' she said, trying to keep her voice even.

'Not a good — ! But . . . but what about the prestige associated with it? Quite apart from the money we'd get from a name-licensing agreement, think about all the free publicity!'

But her mind was racing, trying to come up with a way to avoid having anything to do with Ben. And she felt guilty, because for once she was putting her own interests before those of the company. 'Yes, yes, that's all well and good,' she said, sounding sharper than intended. 'But . . . but how do we know that we'd be associating ourselves with the right kind of magazine? What if the magazine were suddenly to fold? Would we *really* want to associate our name with failure?'

She couldn't meet his gaze, but saw from the corner of her eye that he was frowning at her. 'That's a very negative attitude,' he said mildly. 'Not like you at all.'

'I'm only trying to be realistic about it.'

'Of course. But just supposing the magazine was a great success — a fairly safe bet, I'd say, if Independent International's previous track-record is anything to go by. Would we want to give such a great opportunity to one of our competitors — Malcolm Bradbury over at Yours, for example?'

She shook her head and shrugged, but made no response. Colin was right, of course. Beau Monde would probably never get a better opportunity to elevate its profile. But how could Dani work alongside Ben after all that had happened between them? It would be impossible.

'Look, at least check up on the magazine market before you say no,' Colin said reasonably. 'Ring this fellow Daley, if you like, have a chat with him, sound him out first-hand — '

She forced herself to nod agreeably. 'All right, I'll . . . I'll give it some thought this afternoon, if I have the time, and then we'll see.'

All through the rest of the day Dani continued to deal with her heavy workload, searching in vain for peace of mind as the hours ticked by. At three o'clock that afternoon the telephone on her desk buzzed. 'Yes?'

'Oh, Miss McMasters. I've got David Mason on the line for you.'

'Put him through, will you, Susan?'

A moment later David's voice came into her ear. 'Hello, Dani? I hope I'm not disturbing you.'

'No, not at all.'

'Oh, good. It's just that I've been plugging away at some new designs all day but the wretched things just won't co-operate. I thought perhaps it might help if we could talk them through, maybe over a meal tonight? That is, unless you're otherwise engaged — ?'

'No, no, I think I'd like that,' she replied. She meant it, too. Her only alternative was a quiet and lonely night indoors with only her unhappy thoughts for company. And if it helped David to focus his ideas, then it would be of benefit to both of them.

'Great! Shall I pick you up at, say, seven o'clock?'

'Seven will be fine.'

★ ★ ★

At seven o'clock exactly David Mason collected Dani from her flat and whisked her off to a softly-lit French restaurant not too far away. The atmosphere was warm and relaxing, and as they sipped their pre-dinner drinks, Dani felt the tension of the day finally ebbing out of her.

'So — how was your day?' David asked conversationally. Dani had always enjoyed his boyish enthusiasm, but tonight he seemed to be in even higher spirits than usual.

She considered before answering. 'Busy,' she finally decided.

'What would Colin do without you, eh?' he asked. 'What would *any* of us do without you, come to that?' He raised his glass. 'Long may you continue to enrich us with your presence, that's what I say.'

She was rather taken aback. 'Why, David — how sweet of you.'

They ordered their meal and continued to chat about general topics over their main course, an authentic, and thus delicious, *coq au vin*. At last Dani asked David about the problems he was having with his new designs.

He frowned. 'Problems?'

'Yes. On the phone this afternoon

you said your ideas just wouldn't . . . how did you put it? Oh yes — they wouldn't 'co-operate'.'

'Oh, yes. That's right.' In the intimate golden candlelight he looked sheepish. 'Well, actually I think that maybe I was letting my sketches get the better of me. No matter how much I fiddled with them, I just couldn't seem to fully realize the styles I was trying to create. So I phoned you.'

'And?'

He shrugged and swallowed another mouthful of chicken. 'And I guess all I needed was a break from the drawing-board, because when I went back to it, everything just fell into place.'

'It happens that way sometimes,' Dani replied.

But inside she felt the first stirrings of disquiet, because it was becoming increasingly obvious to her that David's request to talk his design problems through over dinner was little more than a childish ruse to get her to go out with him.

She chewed on her food without really tasting it. David was a sweet young man, but the operative word was *young*. It was true that only four or five years separated them, but for all they had in common beyond the world of fashion, the gap might just as well be twice that.

Still, that was only one reason for Dani's sudden disquiet. To mix business with pleasure — pleasure in the way that *David* probably meant it — could well spell the end of their professional relationship, and Dani dearly did not want that to happen. In any case, he did not yet possess the qualities she admired in a man — those qualities she had found in such abundance within Ben.

There! Again her thoughts had returned to him! Was there no escaping the effect he had on her?

'Dani?'

'Uh . . . I'm sorry, David. What were you saying?'

'I was just asking what you

thought of the chicken?'

Her smile couldn't quite mask her discomfort. 'It's delicious.'

As the evening wore on, Dani began to feel more and more uncomfortable. David's flattery was outrageous, his admiration of her embarrassing. Over coffee, Dani decided that even a quiet night in with only her own troubles for company would have been preferable.

At last David paid the bill and they stepped out into the darkness. She felt the pressure of his hand against the small of her back as he guided her across the pavement. Getting into his car, he asked her if she would like to go on elsewhere, perhaps to a quiet country pub or even a disco.

She shook her head. 'No thank you, David,' she said in a gentle but firm voice. 'The meal was lovely, but I really ought to call it a night. I've got another busy day tomorrow, and I need my sleep.'

'All right,' he said, obviously disappointed. 'If you're sure.'

They drove back through the brisk April night mostly in silence. Once or twice David suggested they make a habit of these little evenings, if she were agreeable, but she remained non-committal.

By the time they reached her apartment block, it became obvious by the sudden dip in his usually buoyant nature that he'd realized that their relationship would never progress beyond its present level. Business was one thing; friendship, too. But Dani was not looking for romance.

'Thanks for a lovely evening,' she said as he put the car in neutral and listened to the quiet idling of the engine.

He stared at her, his face pale in the harsh glow of a nearby street lamp. 'Thank you for the pleasure of your company.'

She quickly opened the door and climbed out before she had to face the embarrassment of a goodnight kiss, but paused once, on the gravel drive, to wave him goodbye. He waved back, sadness all too clear on his young face, then put the car into gear and screeched off into the night.

Dani sighed, unable to shake off the irrational feeling that somehow she had let him down. What had gone wrong with her life? Why was it so full of unhappiness?

As she turned and began to walk along the drive, she caught a movement from the corner of her eye and gave a small, startled gasp as she recognized Ben standing just to the right of the front door.

At once she felt panic rising inside her. Although he dominated her thoughts, she wanted only to avoid him. She felt embarrassed by the way she had behaved the previous day; more embarrassed still because this man, who now might just as well be a stranger to her, knew her so well.

Somehow she forced herself to continue walking up to the building. He just stood there, watching her draw nearer. She felt compelled to meet his gaze, and marvelled at the hypnotic intensity he was still able to radiate. He was wearing tailored blue jeans and a grey jacket over a black turtle-neck sweater. His long, lean face was serious, his chin blued with a faint dusting of stubble, exactly as it had been all those years before.

She fought valiantly to calm her beating heart and bring her swimming senses back to calmer shores. 'What are you doing here?' she asked ungraciously when no more than ten feet separated them.

He chose to overlook her bad manners, which only served to make her feel worse. 'I've come to talk,' he said mildly.

'I didn't think there was anything left to say.'

At last he gave some sign that her attitude was irritating him. 'All right, then — forget it. Forget *everything*.' And he brushed past her, heading for his car, which was parked on the other side of the narrow lane.

She watched him go, hating herself for behaving as she had. She noticed the slight limp in his right leg that was possibly the only physical reminder of that terrible period in his life after the coma. Then, before it was too late to stop him from leaving, she said, 'Wait . . . please.'

He came to a halt, just stood there for a while, staring out into the surrounding darkness, then slowly turned to face her, his shadowed face unreadable. 'Yes?'

'How . . . how long have you been waiting?' she asked, moderating her tone. 'Here, I mean, for me to come home?'

He allowed a brief smile to touch his lips as he walked back to her. 'A couple of hours. I tried ringing you at first, but got no reply. So I came over, just in case you were at home but ignoring the phone.' He turned his dusty blue eyes up to the building before them. 'This is a nice place. You have good neighbours. One of them, an old fellow with a large stick of wood, saw me hanging around and nearly clobbered me across the head!'

She smiled. 'Oh, that'll be Mr Berner. He's become very wary of strangers just lately. I . . . I had a break-in a couple of days ago.'

'I know, he told me. He also told me you'd gone out for the evening. That's how I knew to wait.' He nodded towards the road, where David had been parked just a few minutes before. 'Boyfriend?' he asked.

Before she could form a reply, he caught the flare of warning in her hazel eyes and held out his hands, palms up. 'All right, all right, I'm sorry. None of my business.'

She sighed. This verbal sparring-match was ridiculous. And the effect he was having on her was most disconcerting. 'What . . . what is it that you wanted to talk about?' she asked.

'All sorts of things,' he replied vaguely. 'But I'd sooner not discuss them out here in the open. It's a bit undignified, wouldn't you say?'

She had to make a decision. Should she allow him inside? But then again, why not? The years might have changed him in some ways, but basically he was still the same Ben; that's why, even now, she was finding his very presence intoxicating.

'All right,' she said, trying her best to sound formal and detached.

She punched in her security number and he followed her across the hallway to her front door. Soon they were in her living-room, and she was studying him surreptitiously. He looked weary in the stronger light, but maybe that, too, was a legacy of his accident.

'You, ah . . . you'll have to excuse me if I don't say much,' she said, deciding that it would be wisest to erect some sort of invisible barrier between them, and choosing sarcasm as her best defence. 'It's just that I'm not used to conversing with dead men.'

He ignored the jibe. 'I'll come straight to the point, then,' he said. 'I'm here primarily to apologize for all the unhappiness I've brought you.' He snorted. 'Oh, I know that an apology must sound ridiculous in the circumstance, but I just don't know what else I can do to make it up to you. To be honest, I don't think there *is* anything I can do. In retrospect, it was stupid of me to concoct such a crazy notion, but at the time I guess I wanted to be so noble and selfless about everything . . . ' His eyes came up to her face. 'Well, I suppose you know what they say about the road to hell . . . '

Dani looked away from him. 'I . . . I don't really think there's very much I can say about it myself, Ben . . . Matthew . . . whatever.' She shook her head. 'I don't believe I can find the words to describe how I feel about everything that's happened.'

He nodded his understanding. 'Well, I won't trouble you any longer. I just wanted to say I was sorry.'

She felt emptiness well up inside her, and hated herself for wishing he would stay. 'I'm sorry, too,' she said in a small voice. 'For slapping you the way I did.'

He reached up and rubbed his cheek. 'You had every right,' he replied. 'But you sure do pack a wallop!'

When she returned his smile some of the tension left the air. 'Would you . . . could I get you a coffee before you go?' she asked.

Much to her relief, he nodded. 'Thanks. I'd like that.'

She hurried into the kitchen and switched on the kettle. When she returned to the living-room he said, 'Do you mind if I take my jacket off? It's all right — I don't intend to outstay my welcome. It's just that I've been dressed up like a tailor's dummy all day, and I never was one for suits and ties.'

'Yes, I remember,' she said quietly. She told him to make himself comfortable, still struggling mightily to maintain some degree of detachment. 'Do you miss your photography?' she asked, straightening some cushions.

'A lot,' he said, sitting down. 'I still

snap away at weekends, whenever I can, but it's not the same.'

'Still, you've come a long way.'

'And so have *you*. I had no idea you'd gone over to the managerial side of the fashion business, and even less that you'd gone to work for Beau Monde . . . '

She glanced over at him. One question above all others was uppermost in her mind, and although she had to ask it, she was dreading the answer. Looking away from him again, she said lightly, as if the matter were of no real consequence, 'So . . . tell me all about yourself. You must be married by now. Do you have a family?'

'I never married,' he said quietly.

'Pressure of work, I expect,' she said, sounding him out.

He made no reply.

She hid her reaction well. 'I'll . . . I'll just go and fetch the coffee.'

'What about you?' he called as she left the room. 'I know you still use your single name, but that doesn't mean anything these days. Lots of married women do. Did you ever, ah, you know . . . ' He faltered. 'Did you ever find anyone else?'

She returned carrying two steaming mugs. 'There you are,' she said, avoiding a direct reply because she was too embarrassed to admit that she had always held true to her promise to be his for eternity.

He decided not to push the point. 'I suppose you know I've been in correspondence with Colin Howard over a magazine we're intending to launch,' he said, steering the conversation onto safer ground.

'Yes. We were only discussing it this morning. Colin seems to think it will be a marvellous opportunity for us if we allow you to use our company name.'

'So do I. But do I sense a little reservation on your part?'

Her sigh was expressive. 'It's certainly a good idea,' she admitted.

'But . . . ?'

'But how could we work together

after all this time, Ben? Just imagine how awkward and embarrassing it would be — for both of us.'

He took a sip of coffee. 'I guess it would, wouldn't it? But couldn't we overcome that? For the good of Beau Monde and Independent International?'

'I don't know,' she said, '*Could* we?'

His eyes assumed a faraway look, as though he were remembering all the times they'd spent together in their previous lives. 'Maybe not,' he said at last. 'Well . . . I'll contact Colin first thing in the morning, withdraw from negotiations before things go too far.'

She nodded, but there was no real sense of relief in her. Just the opposite, in fact. She had betrayed Colin and his company just to get her own selfish way.

Ben checked his wrist-watch. 'Look, I really ought to be going. It's late, and I've taken up enough of your time.' As he rose to his feet, he winced.

'Are you all right?' she asked with concern.

He nodded and reached for his jacket. 'Sure. It's just that, ever since the accident, I tend to tire easily towards the end of the day, and my muscles stiffen up. I'll be as right as rain after a good night's sleep.'

He moved over to the living-room door, then turned back to face her. 'There's just one other thing before I go,' he said.

Her heart resumed its runaway pounding as she wondered what it was, and how she would react to it. 'Yes?'

'Yesterday afternoon, just before you left the cottage, you accused me of sending someone to spy on you. What did you mean by that?'

'Oh, come on, Ben — '

'I mean it, Dani,' he said earnestly. 'Oh, sure, I always used to make a point of asking Dad if he'd heard from you, and what you'd been up to. But I'd never send anyone to *spy* on you.'

She ran her searching gaze across his face, and saw only genuine concern and puzzlement there. 'You . . . you mean you *didn't* employ someone to follow me?' she asked, fighting an impulse to shiver.

'Of course not!' He reached out and took her by the arms. This time it was he who scanned *her* face. 'Do you mean to say that someone *has* been following you?'

She nodded.

'Are you sure?'

'Well, almost. It . . . It started on Tuesday morning. At least that's when I first became *aware* of it. Someone in a white car, following me everywhere I went. He even followed me to your father's cottage yesterday!'

He eased his urgent grip on her. 'I swear to God I had nothing to do with it.'

'I . . . I just assumed . . . I mean, your father said you were concerned about me after I fainted on Monday — '

'I was. I *am*.'

'He said you kept wondering if I were all right afterwards, so I just assumed that you'd hired someone to check up for you.'

He looked grim and thoughtful. 'Maybe you should call the police about this,' he suggested.

'But I don't have any *proof*, Ben. It could just be coincidence. A different car each time.' A faint, rueful smile played across her lips. 'This has been quite a week, don't forget. I've had my mind elsewhere.'

He nodded. 'But what if it's *not* coincidence? What if this burglary of yours is all tied in with it somehow?'

Now she could not help but shiver. 'You're beginning to frighten me,' she said, only half joking.

'Good,' he replied. 'You *should* be frightened. Until we sort this business out once and for all, you should take it all very seriously.'

He was right, of course. She led him through to the front door, making a mental note to check all the locks and windows before going to bed.

Suddenly she became aware that he

was staring down at her, and felt heat rush to her face.

'It's been good to see you again,' he said sincerely. 'To talk to you, and see you smile.'

She flustered like a schoolgirl. 'Thank you for coming over to apologize.'

For a moment she was reminded of that night when he had first confessed his love for her. There was something hauntingly similar in the soft buzz of feeling between them now. She looked up at him, into his eyes, and felt his hands slide up onto her shoulders. This time her shiver was one of pleasure. Then his serious face began to lower towards her own, and she knew that even after all this time, she would be happy to drown in his embrace.

But suddenly panic overwhelmed her. She had loved the old Ben, yes, but what did she know of the new? And, come to that, after all these years, what did he really know about her?

Abruptly she pulled away from him, face still flushed, heart still pounding, curiously disappointed that their kiss had not taken place, and annoyed by her own fears.

He took a step away from her, so that she would not feel threatened by his presence. 'I'm sorry,' he said, clearing his throat. 'I had no right to — '

'*I'm* sorry,' she said, not meeting his eyes. 'It's just that . . . ' It was no good; she must be totally, painfully honest for both of them. 'Ben — we're not the same people we used to be. We're strangers to each other now. Old friends who've each moved on in different directions. You see that, don't you?'

She thought her words had caused a flicker of hurt to pass across his face, but maybe she only imagined it.

Finally he nodded. 'Perhaps you're right,' he agreed softly. 'Goodnight, Dani. And remember — take care.'

8

Dani spent a restless night dreaming about Ben. In the cold greyness of dawn she lay remembering how close they had come to kissing, and regretted the fact that she had allowed a sudden attack of panic to shatter the moment. The warmth of his skin, the scent of his cologne . . . even just the memory of them were enough to make her skin tingle.

And yet, at the same time, she was glad that their lips had not met. Because in no way would a kiss between them have been a casual thing. It would have been a firm, unspoken commitment. And how could Dani commit herself to man she no longer knew?

Restless, she rose early and showered, then dressed and drank coffee before slipping into her jacket and preparing for the journey to work.

As she crunched across the drive to her car, she carefully scanned her surroundings for any sign of the mysterious white car. For here was another problem to vex her. Who was the driver? For whom was he working, if not Ben? Why was he following her, and *was* he connected to the burglary in some way?

She had arranged weeks ago to spend the coming weekend with her parents in Reading, and realized now that the change of scene couldn't come soon enough. In view of what had already happened, she was, of course, reluctant to leave her flat unattended, but Mr and Mrs Berner had promised to keep an eye on it for her, and call the police at the first hint of trouble.

That day passed much like the previous one, with Dani determined to banish all thought of Ben from her mind by immersing herself in her work. In those odd moments between jobs, however, her mind strayed back to the previous evening, how tired he had looked and yet how polite he had remained despite the discomfort of his aching muscles.

For the first time, she stepped outside of herself in order to view what had happened all those years before from a different perspective. But she knew she could never imagine how badly Ben must have taken the news that he would never use his limbs again. Had he given in to despair? He must have, at first.

'I guess I wanted to be so noble and selfless about everything,' he'd told her when referring to his decision to 'die', and spare her the burden of looking after him.

Now she realized how much that decision must have torn him apart, and how truly noble he *had* been to go through with it, for just when he'd needed all the love in the world, he had chosen to free her of all her commitments to him . . .

She stared down at the paperwork

she was supposed to be dealing with, but couldn't seem to take in the meaning of the typed words. Now her imaginings had moved on, to picture those long, agonizing months directly after he had recovered from his coma. She winced just at the thought of the pain he must have suffered, the physiotherapy he had endured, the operations he had undergone. The determination and courage he had doubtless shown only increased the love she had never really lost for him.

It occurred to her that she should phone him. She doubted that they would ever meet again, but nevertheless she wanted him to know that she understood his motives now, and admired the spirit in which he had acted. Telling him that she felt no bitterness towards him might go part of the way to expunging some of the guilt he obviously still felt. And by laying their differences to rest, she might also set *herself* free from the invisible chains that still bound her to him.

Colin had left 'Matthew Daley's' letter on her desk. Now, running her eyes across it, she located Independent International's telephone number beneath the company logo, picked up her receiver and dialled. Her heart was beating madly and her mouth was desert-dry, but she knew that it was the right thing to do.

After a few seconds, the call was answered by a switchboard girl. 'Hello, Independent International Magazines. Can I help you?'

Dani scanned the letterhead. 'Extension 491, please.'

There was a click. Ringing in her ear. Then another female voice said, 'Good-morning, Mr Daley's office.'

'Good-morning. I wonder if I might have a word with Mr, ah, Daley, if he's available?'

'I'm sorry. He's just left the office.'

'Oh. Will he be back later, do you know?'

'He won't be in again until Monday week, I'm afraid. Can I help at all, or would you care to leave a message?'

Dani's heart sank. 'No . . . no, it's all right. It . . . it wasn't important.'

She replaced the handset. She had so wanted to hear his voice again, but even that small opportunity seemed lost to her now. It wouldn't be the same to ring him in a week's time. Maybe she ought to write instead, provided she could find, or remember, Brian's full address.

Dani left work at five o'clock that afternoon, drove home to collect the small case she had packed for the weekend, then set out for the drive to Reading. Although she kept a wary eye on her rear-view mirror, she saw no sign of the white car, and wondered if perhaps it *had* just been coincidence after all.

It was even better to go home than she'd imagined. To be surrounded by so many familiar faces, sights and sounds offered her the comfort for which she had been searching so long. Almost as soon as she arrived, her spirits lifted.

She had lived alone for such a long time that she had almost forgotten the joys of family life.

Her parents were keen to hear all her news, and while she tried to cram in as much as she could, she deliberately played down the burglary so as not to alarm them unduly. As for Ben . . . She decided not to mention him at all.

They seemed to spend nearly all their time laughing. Just having their daughter home for the weekend was as much a tonic for Dani's parents as it was for her. They went shopping together, for walks in the nearby forest, watched television and chatted late into the night. It was the most relaxing period Dani felt she had ever spent anywhere.

But Saturday became Sunday with a speed that surprised her. The weekend had flown past, and she was reluctant for it to end. It was so nice to be home, protected from the unfairness of life in the real world, that she felt she would have been happy to stay there forever.

But that, of course, was impossible,

and so it was that Dani re-packed her weekend case with a heavy heart late on Sunday afternoon, in preparation for the journey back to her lonely flat.

★ ★ ★

By the time she arrived for work on Monday morning, the weekend might just as well have been a dream, because Dani was plunged back in at the deep end almost at once.

'Trouble,' Kate Allison warned as she followed her boss into her office.

Dani eyed the younger, dark-haired girl expectantly. 'Oh?'

'Redbridge Fabrics,' Kate replied, naming one of their leading material suppliers. 'They were on the phone to me first thing this morning. It appears that there's going to be a delay in filling our current order before the end of June.'

'Oh no!'

'Oh *yes*, I'm afraid. They're in the middle of an industrial dispute, or something. Until they can settle it, no new fabrics are being produced, and no existing stock is being allowed to leave the factory.'

Dani sighed, set down her briefcase and took off her jacket. 'I'd better call them back. We need that order desperately if we're to get the bulk of the collection we showed last week into our stores by the autumn.'

'Don't I know it,' Kate said with feeling. 'But short of sitting around the negotiating table with the unions, what can you do about it?'

Dani shrugged. 'Apply some pressure on the management to find a quick solution to their problem?'

Kate grimaced. 'Sooner you than me.'

'Any other bombshells I ought to know about?' Dani asked, sitting down.

'Yes — *two*.'

Both girls turned their attention to the door as Colin Howard stalked in, his usually genial manner now replaced by a dark and angry scowl.

'What is it, Colin?' Dani asked, surprised by his uncharacteristic demeanour.

'Well, *this*, for a start,' he replied, throwing a letter onto her desk. Dani saw the Independent International logo and swallowed nervously. So; Ben had been as good as his word. As if to confirm it, Colin said, 'Can you imagine the nerve of this fellow Daley? He contacts me right out of the blue and asks if we'd be interested in linking our company with his magazine, and then, before we can say yes or no, he writes again to tell me that he's decided not to take the wretched proposal any further!'

He ran a hand through his greying hair. 'You know what's happened, don't you? We've spent so much time dithering over our reply that he's got fed up and gone elsewhere!'

'Well, we don't know that for a fact,' Kate said placatingly.

'It's all my fault,' Dani said quietly, before she could help herself.

Colin eyed her sidelong. 'What's that?'

She realized what she'd said. 'I, ah . . . if I'd been a little more enthusiastic when you first mentioned it to me on Friday — '

Some of Colin's anger evaporated, and he smiled. 'Oh, you can't blame yourself,' he said with such understanding that she quickly felt even more guilty than she had to begin with. 'No, I expect this fellow Daley just ran out of patience — or received a better offer from someone else.' He picked up the letter and scanned it one last time. 'Still,' he said softly, 'I can't say I'm not disappointed, because I am. I rather fancied the idea of linking Beau Monde with an up-market magazine. Why, I might even have been able to write one or two features for it myself.'

His cheeks suddenly coloured at the admission.

Seated at her desk, Dani began to feel even more wretched. How could she have hurt Colin in such a way after all the kindness he had shown her over the years? Perhaps she should have a word with him in private, and confess everything. But would that only make the matter worse?

'What was the other bombshell?' Kate asked into the silence.

'Eh?' said Colin, looking up from the letter in his hands.

'You said you had *two* bombshells for us,' Kate reminded him. 'I dread to think what the second one is.'

'Oh, it gets even *better*,' Colin said irritably. 'I've just come off the phone from David Mason, who rang to tell me that, for reasons best known to himself, he's decided to sever all connections with Beau Monde and go to work for our competitors!'

'*What?*'

'Who?' asked Kate.

'He didn't specify.'

'Well . . . *why*? I always thought he was happy with us.'

'He was. But something has obviously upset him — though I'm darned if I know what it is.'

Dani had a shrewd notion as to the

answer, but didn't want to voice it in case she was wrong. She was almost certain, however, that it had something to do with their dinner-date the previous Thursday — and the fact that she had doggedly resisted all his attempts at romance.

'Why don't *I* have a word with him?' she suggested.

'If he wouldn't speak to me — ' Colin began.

'That's a good idea,' Kate interrupted. 'Dani's always got on well with David. He might be more willing to open up to her than he would be to the rest of us.' She turned to Dani. 'Shall I get him on the phone for you?'

Dani shook her head. 'No, I think it would be best if I went to see him in person.'

'What about Redbridge Fabrics?'

'I'll see to them,' Colin decided. 'Trying to keep David from leaving the fold is more important right now. Designers like him are the life-blood of our business. Without him, we'd have no clothes to sell in our shops — and no need for Redbridge Fabrics at *all*.'

★   ★   ★

As Dani travelled down to the rear car-park in the softly-lit elevator, she wondered how best she should deal with David. Firmly, or with sympathy? It was a difficult decision. She did not want him to think that she was attempting to dominate him any more than she wanted him to feel that he was being patronized. But neither did she want him to possibly jeopardize his entire career over such a small and insignificant matter.

As she hurried across to her car, she concluded that it would probably be best to play their forthcoming encounter by ear. She did not want for them to argue, and she had no wish to tie him to Beau Monde if he was moving on for a definite purpose. But if, as she suspected, he was dissociating himself from the company just because he no longer thought it possible that they could work together —

She switched on the ignition and waited while the engine warmed up. Suddenly she saw how similar this situation was to the one she had just been through with Ben. She had not believed it possible that *they* could work together. And, under the circumstances, she still did not.

But that was only because they had shared so much in the past, and each held so many memories of the other. With herself and David, it was entirely different. At no time had they ever enjoyed anything but a happy and mutually-rewarding business relationship.

It occurred to her that if he was made to realize that, she might yet talk some good sense into him, and heal whatever rift had developed between them.

The young designer had a small flat in Chelsea. It was not really far from the office, but as soon as Dani got caught up in the morning traffic, she realized that the journey was going to take her far longer than it should.

Before long her speed had slowed to a crawl. Up ahead, a lorry had shed its load, not helping matters one bit. Amid all the impatient blaring of car horns, she spied a side-street just a short way up on her left, and when she was close enough, turned into it.

It felt good to be moving again, and leaving all the noisy chaos behind her. Now, if only she could just find a route across town that would help her avoid any more traffic jams —

Suddenly she caught sight of a white car in her rear-view mirror, and experienced a nasty stab of alarm. Was it *the* white car? It couldn't be . . . *could* it?

As she tried to concentrate on her driving, she also searched her memory for any details that might confirm that the car behind her now was indeed the same one that had been haunting her for the past week. She realized despondently that she should have tried to identify its make, and made a note of its licence number, and regretted the oversight.

But perhaps she was panicking for no good reason. After all, the city must be teeming with cars of the same type and colour. She comforted herself with the knowledge that it *could* still be coincidence, and nothing more.

She came to the end of the side-street and indicated that she was going to turn right. The traffic here was quite light, so she had no trouble in keeping an eye on the car behind her.

It, too, turned right.

Now her nerve was beginning to crumble. For every positive thought she came up with, another part of her mind whispered a negative one. What if she *were* being followed? Was there a perfectly reasonable explanation, or a sinister one?

She took her next left, in danger now of becoming hopelessly lost in a maze of back-streets. The white car also turned left, keeping some two hundred feet behind her.

Who was the driver? Why was he so determined to keep her in sight? She realized that she must discover his identity and purpose, or go mad with speculation.

Swallowing nervously, she decided that, like it or not, she was going to have to confront him head-on in order to get her answers.

She indicated and turned left again, into a narrow one-way street. It was, she realized, ideal for her purpose. Another jolt of fear ran through her as the white car appeared in her rear-view mirror, still roughly two hundred feet behind her.

Now she had no doubt at all that she was being followed, for it was unlikely that any motorist would wish to take such a meandering route from one place to another.

She reduced her speed, slowly allowing the white car to creep nearer in the mirror. She realized that she was being impulsive and, perhaps, foolish. But her mind was made up. This mystery-man had followed her for one entire week — and added to all the other pressures in her life, that was one entire week too long.

By now the driver of the white car had realized that he was gaining on Dani's ice-green Metro. But before he, too, could reduce his speed and fall back, Dani brought her car to a halt and quickly climbed out.

With butterflies in her tummy, she began to hurry back along the street, trying to see beyond the wind-screen of the other car and identify the driver. 'Who are you?' she called, trying to keep her voice steady and full of authority. 'Why are you following me?'

The white car was no more than fifty feet away now. It bounced to a halt. It could not go forward, because Dani's car was blocking the way, and the one-way street was too narrow for it to turn round. And neither could the car reverse, because a third car was now blocking it from behind.

'Who *are* you?' Dani repeated, coming closer and wishing that her anger would overcome her fear completely.

At last she could see the driver. He appeared to be a smallish man, with a thin, pale face and dark, shifty-looking eyes. She didn't recognize him at all. But she saw alarm on his face, and that helped to quell her own fear a little.

'Why are you following me?' she demanded again.

He shook his head, attempting an awkward smile in order to calm her down. 'I . . . I don't know what you're talking about,' he protested.

'You've been following me off and on for the past week,' she said, coming to a stop beside the driver's door. 'Why? Tell me!'

The thin-faced man licked his lips. 'You've got the wrong man, lady. I haven't done anything. Now move along. You're obstructing the traffic.'

As if to underline his words, Dani heard a car door slam, and realized that the driver of the car behind his was coming over, probably to voice *his* complaints about her behaviour as well.

But to her utter surprise, she heard a familiar voice say, 'You heard Miss McMasters' questions. *Answer* them!'

Dani looked up at the man now standing beside her and felt such a rush of relief just at the sight of him that she had to blink grateful tears from her eyes. '*Ben!*'

But Ben wasn't looking at her. His dusty blue eyes were burning into the driver of the white car, who was now squirming with obvious discomfort.

'All right,' Ben went on. 'I'll give you a choice. You can either answer *our* questions — or those of the police.'

Panic appeared on the small man's face as he peered up at them. 'I don't know what — '

'I should warn you,' Ben said. 'I have all the evidence I need to exercise my citizen's right of arrest. While you've been following Miss McMasters here, *I've* been following *you*, so don't try to deny it any longer!'

The small man's resolve seemed to crumble at last. 'No police,' he said. 'I don't want no trouble with the police — '

'Then answer our questions,' Dani said, her mind still in a whirl. 'Who are you? Why have you been following me?'

The man turned sullen. He knew he could evade the truth no longer. 'My name's Joe Taylor,' he mumbled. 'I'm a registered private investigator.'

'You've got proof of that, I suppose,' Ben snapped tightly.

Grudgingly, the small man took out a wallet, from which he extracted a copy of his licence, which also contained his picture, and his driver's licence, which confirmed both his name and address.

'Then you've been following me as a job of work?' Dani prompted.

The small man nodded.

'Who hired you?' asked Ben.

'That information's confidential — '

'It's us or the police, remember.'

Joe Taylor weighed everything up in

his mind. 'If I tell you,' he said, 'will you let me go? I'll drop the case, I swear it. But I . . . I don't want no trouble with the police.'

Ben glanced down at Dani. 'Well?' he asked. 'It's up to you. I'll make a note of this fellow's details, so if it starts up again, we'll know exactly who to blame, and where to find him.'

Dani didn't even hesitate. 'All right. Tell us the name of your client.'

★　★　★

'Malcolm Bradbury!'

Ben studied her closely across the small corner table. It was twenty minutes later, and they were certain that Joe Taylor had told them as much as he knew before they'd let him go.

As the private detective drove away, Ben had peered down at Dani's grim profile. She had looked as white as chalk, still understandably stunned by the morning's surprising events.

'Come on,' he'd said gently, reaching

out to fold a supportive arm about her shoulders. 'I think you could probably use a sweet cup of tea before we go any further. I know a little Italian coffee-shop just around the corner. Let's park our cars and talk this through.'

She had looked up at him. 'What? Oh, yes . . . yes. I *do* feel a bit shaken up.'

Now he watched her carefully through the steam rising off her cup. The coffee-shop, in between its breakfast and lunchtime crowds, was peaceful now. 'Malcolm Bradbury,' he repeated. 'The name obviously means something to you. What is he, an ex-boyfriend or something?'

Dani raised her cup and summoned a sour smile. 'Hardly. He owns a rival High Street clothing chain called Yours. For the last couple of years he's been trying to lure me away from Beau Monde. The last time — just a couple of weeks ago — he took my refusal almost as a personal insult. I was glad to leave his office.'

Ben nodded. 'From what Joe Taylor just told us, it doesn't seem as if Bradbury meant you any real harm. He only wanted to find out where you were going every day, and why. Would it be safe to assume he was hoping that you would lead him to all these marvellous young designers you've discovered, do you think? Perhaps he thought he might have better luck poaching them away from BM than he did with you.'

'I believe you're right,' she agreed. 'In fact, I'm almost certain he's already approached the very designer I was just on my way to see!'

'Then the sooner we get to *him* and explain the depths to which his prospective new employer will go to to recruit new talent, the better.'

She arched a questioning eyebrow, feeling safe and happy in his presence. '*We?* And that reminds me — I still haven't thanked you for helping me yet. How *did* you know where to find me?'

His smile was rueful. 'I wasn't just bluffing when I told Taylor I'd been following him. I *had*. I didn't like the idea that someone might be spying on you, and I knew you were too level-headed to let your imagination run away with you.'

'So you took a week's leave from work and set yourself up to follow Taylor!'

He nodded, then frowned. 'How did *you* know I'd taken a week off?'

She blushed. 'I . . . Look, you're probably right, Ben. The sooner I get to see David Mason, the better. But thank you once again. I really appreciate your kindness.'

He put his right hand over hers. 'Just because I disappeared from your life for six years, it doesn't mean to say that I don't still care.'

She avoided his gaze, flustering. 'I . . . I must go.'

'We'll go together,' he said firmly. 'Because, whether you realize it or not, this little business isn't over yet.'

She frowned up at him, wondering what he could possibly mean.

★ ★ ★

They took Ben's car, and following her directions, he drove Dani to David Mason's flat, agreeing to wait outside while she went up to see him alone.

The building was one of those white-stone, Georgian-style houses which had long since been converted into separate apartments. David lived on the second floor. Dani let herself through the front door and began to climb the stairs, wondering what kind of welcome she would receive at the top.

When she reached David's door, she drew in a steadying breath, then thumbed the doorbell. For a moment she didn't think she would get any response. Then the door opened and David stood there, surprise — and embarrassment — showing on his tanned face.

'Oh — it's you!'

She nodded, offering him a tentative smile. 'I'm sorry if I've disturbed you.

I should have phoned first, I suppose, but . . . Can I come in for a moment?'

He eyed her with suspicion. 'Why?' he asked with a trace of half-hearted belligerence.

'Well, I think we should talk,' she said simply.

The distrust never left his face. 'Talk? What is there left to talk *about*?'

She allowed a firmer tone to enter her voice. 'Well, about your reasons for wanting to leave Beau Monde, for one thing,' she said. 'And about the friendship between us that I believe is too important to lose just because of a misunderstanding. And . . .'

His eyes narrowed. 'And?'

She took a deep breath. 'And about a rather nasty piece of work by the name of Malcolm Bradbury,' she said.

Recognition of the name flickered across his face. 'You, ah . . . I think you'd better come in, then.'

★ ★ ★

Dani returned to the car half an hour later.

'At last,' said Ben. But there was no real criticism in his voice. He twisted around, watching her settle herself beside him, then asked, 'Well — how did it go with your designer friend? Did you sort everything out?'

She smiled, and realized that the action was becoming increasingly easy for her. 'Yes,' she said. 'Everything.'

It was true, too. As they had suspected, David *had* been approached by Malcolm Bradbury, and, still feeling foolish for attempting to take his and Dani's friendship beyond the platonic, David had decided that it might be best to accept his offer and go to work at Yours.

But fortunately, Dani's visit had changed all that. As he listened to her story, David began to realize exactly what sort of man he would be going to work for; and realize also that it *was* possible for him to still enjoy her company without feeling embarrassed

214

by his one abortive try at romance.

Soon the ice in his tone and manner had thawed, and Dani left his flat in buoyant spirits. She had stopped David from possibly making a bad career move, and patched up their ailing friendship. But now, as she stared across at the man she loved, she wondered what he had meant when he'd told her that this business wasn't over yet.

She asked him, but he remained close-mouthed. 'Just trust me,' he said. 'And tell me how best to get to Malcolm Bradbury's office from here.'

'Ben — ' she warned.

'*Trust* me,' he repeated, meeting her eyes. 'There won't be any trouble, I promise you. But I've got a feeling that there's still one last piece of this jigsaw that needs to be slotted together.'

She searched his face for further clues, but it was obvious that he would say no more. 'All right,' she finally sighed.

He pulled away from the kerb and,

following her directions, drove straight to Bradbury's head office. Parking outside, he turned to study her with a serious expression on his lean, tanned face. 'Now,' he said in a low voice, 'when we finally get to see this fellow Bradbury, I'm going to bluff and guess like crazy, all right? So, whatever you do, try not to look surprised or startled by anything I say.'

'Ben . . . ' she began.

'Come on,' he said, lightening his tone.

At the Yours reception desk, they were told that Malcolm Bradbury was in conference, but Ben had evidently expected that. 'I think you'd better tell him exactly who I am, then,' he told the receptionist in a tone that would brook no argument. 'My name is Ben Tremain — and I am Miss McMasters' legal adviser.'

He might have used a magic password, for as soon as the receptionist rang the information through, she said, 'You're to go straight in.'

Taking Dani by the arm, Ben led her into a plush, well-appointed office. Malcolm Bradbury was standing behind a large desk. He was a small, slim man with dark hair and slightly Mediterranean features, somewhere in his forties.

He tried an exploratory smile on Dani. 'Ah, Miss McMasters. How . . . how nice to see you again — '

'If you don't mind,' Ben interrupted in a brisk and business-like way, 'we'll come straight to the point. I daresay you've already received a call from one Joe Taylor, so you know why we're here.'

Bradbury looked ill at ease. 'I . . . there's been some sort of misunderstanding . . . ' he began.

'I think not,' Ben told him gravely. 'You have committed a number of very serious offences here, Mr Bradbury, as I'm sure Joe Taylor would be only too happy to testify. But we have no wish to bring the matter to court. Bad publicity does no-one any favours.'

Now the managing director of Yours looked puzzled. 'Then what — ?'

'We want your solemn oath to leave Miss McMasters alone in future. Do you understand? She has no wish to work for you, and no desire to be spied upon by your underlings.'

Bradbury licked his lips. 'I — ' He seemed to wither beneath Ben's glare. 'You . . . All right. If you really mean what you say about not taking the matter to court . . . I give you my solemn oath.'

Dani released a sigh — but Ben wasn't finished yet.

'Oh — and one other thing,' he said. 'Miss McMasters suffered a break-in at her flat last week. I would be grateful if you would return whatever it was that you had Joe Taylor steal on your behalf.'

Bradbury's eyes flashed. He opened his mouth to voice a denial, but saw the futility of it. Ben was right; bad publicity would do him no favours at all. Without saying a word, he opened his desk drawer and took out —

'My address-book!' Dani whispered.

'Exactly,' Ben said as if he'd known what Bradbury had stolen all along. He reached over and took it from the other man's hands. 'And if you try to approach any of the designers listed in here . . . ' he cautioned.

'Don't worry — I won't.'

Ben smiled. 'Then I believe that concludes our business, Mr Bradbury. Good-day to you.'

*   *   *

Outside, Dani could not help herself. Such was her sense of admiration for him, she *had* to discard the invisible barriers she had set up between them. 'Ben — that was marvellous! You should have been an actor! Why, even *I* believed you were my legal adviser!'

He smiled modestly. 'Not a bad job of bluffing and guesswork at that, I suppose,' he replied. But there was something subdued in his manner. 'Hop in,' he said, unlocking the passenger-side door. 'I'll drop you back at your car.'

It struck *her* then; that for an hour or so they had been united by a common cause, and that now the problem had been resolved, they were each going their separate ways.

She climbed into the car feeling curiously deflated. It had been so good to be in Ben's company again. It had felt so comfortable and *right*. But how could she tell him that now, after she'd already told him that they were as good as strangers — no more than old friends who had since gone their separate ways?

Ben got into the car beside her and she looked at his profile. Her heart ached for this man who had been her first — and would, without doubt, be her *last* — love. She cleared her throat and he glanced over at her. His eyes reflected his own sadness at their imminent parting.

'Ben,' she said in a small voice.

'Yes?'

'About the letter you sent to Colin,' she said haltingly. 'He . . . he was quite upset that you'd decided to withdraw from negotiations . . . more disappointed than I'd realized.'

'That wasn't my idea,' he pointed out.

'I know. But . . . Is it too late to reconsider, do you think? Do you think it possible that we — the two of us — *could* work together?'

He drew in a deep breath. 'You're the only one who can answer that, Dani. All I can tell you is that the only way the last six years have changed me is to make me love you even more now than I did back then. I *am* the same Ben — apart from my aching muscles and a few crow's-feet around my eyes — and I will never, *ever* love anyone with the same depth and intensity as I love you. As I've *always* loved you.' He paused, watching as tears of joy filled her hazel eyes. '*My* only question is — have the last six years changed *you*?'

She shook her head, unable to speak.

Then she swallowed hard and said, 'No, Ben — I . . . I haven't changed a bit.'

And she went forward into his welcoming arms, eager — and happy — to prove it.

THE END

We do hope that you have enjoyed reading this large print book.

Did you know that all of our titles are available for purchase?

We publish a wide range of high quality large print books including:
Romances, Mysteries, Classics
General Fiction
Non Fiction and Westerns

Special interest titles available in large print are:
The Little Oxford Dictionary
Music Book, Song Book
Hymn Book, Service Book

Also available from us courtesy of Oxford University Press:
Young Readers' Dictionary
(large print edition)
Young Readers' Thesaurus
(large print edition)

For further information or a free brochure, please contact us at:
Ulverscroft Large Print Books Ltd.,
The Green, Bradgate Road, Anstey,
Leicester, LE7 7FU, England.
Tel: (00 44) **0116 236 4325**
Fax: (00 44) **0116 234 0205**

Other titles in the
Linford Romance Library:

PORTRAIT OF LOVE

Margaret McDonagh

Three generations of the Metcalfe family are settled and successful — professionally and personally. Or are they? An unexpected event sparks a chain reaction, bringing challenges to all the family. Loyalties are questioned, foundations rocked. A secret is exposed, unleashing a journey of discovery, combining past memories, present tensions, the promise of lost love and new hope for the future. Can the family embrace the events overtaking them? When the dust settles, will they emerge stronger and more united?